A
Harlequin
Romance

WELCOME

TO THE WONDERFUL WORLD

of Harlequin Romances!

Interesting, informative and entertaining,
each Harlequin Romance portrays an appealing
love story. Harlequin Romances take you
to faraway places — places with real people
facing real love situations — and
you become part of their story.

As publishers of Harlequin Romances, we're extremely
proud of our books (we've been publishing
them since 1954). We're proud also that Harlequin
Romances are North America's most-read
paperback romances.

Eight new titles are released every month and are
sold at nearly all book-selling stores across
Canada and the United States.

A free catalogue listing all available Harlequin Romances
can be yours by writing to the

HARLEQUIN READER SERVICE,
M.P.O. Box 707, Niagara Falls, N.Y. 14302.
Canadian address: Stratford, Ontario, Canada.

or use order coupon at back of book.

We sincerely hope you enjoy reading
this Harlequin Romance.

Yours truly,

THE PUBLISHERS
   Harlequin Romances

THE
CRESCENT MOON

by

ELIZABETH HUNTER

HARLEQUIN BOOKS   TORONTO
WINNIPEG

Original hard cover edition published in 1973
by Mills & Boon Limited.

© Elizabeth Hunter 1973

SBN 373-01758-8

Harlequin edition published February 1974

For
MONICA

Printed in Canada

1758

CHAPTER I

MADELEINE Carvill heaved a great sigh of relief and thought how lucky she was. It was the first time since coming to Istanbul that this aspect of her situation had occurred to her – but then it was also the first time that she had escaped the company of her employer for a few hours. It wasn't that she disliked Ursula Adeney. If anything, she felt rather sorry for her. She was young and pretty, far too young to be widowed and left in charge of the rapidly expanding magazine chain that had previously belonged to her husband. If there was friction between them, the odd impatient word, Madeleine put it down to the fact that Mrs. Adeney was an American and funny little misunderstandings could blow up from nowhere because of the common language that would suddenly diverge disastrously. Take the word "joint". To Madeleine it meant a piece of meat, to Mrs. Adeney it was the hotel where they were staying. Mouldy old joint, she had said, and Madeleine had expressed surprise, her own food having been perfectly cooked and served. In fact Madeleine thought the hotel rather a fine one, but then she had never had much money and Mrs. Ursula Adeney was a very rich young woman indeed.

Madeleine wasn't quite sure what they were doing in Turkey. Mrs. Adeney had been visiting London when the decision had been made and there had been a sudden flurry in the London office of Adeney Publications as they had made the reservations and bought the first class air tickets Mrs. Adeney had demanded be obtained overnight. It was the London manager who had said that Mrs. Adeney ought to have someone to go with her. He had put it very tactfully, or so the gossip in the office had said. Mrs. Adeney might feel inclined to do a couple of articles for the group while she was away? Then Mrs. Adeney must have a secretary with her just in case the muse should come upon her while she was in Istanbul. Even so, Madeleine had been surprised when she had been chosen to accompany Mrs. Adeney. She would have thought the London manager would have chosen somebody older, somebody in fact who could have exercised a measure of restraint over the impulsive whims of the rich, pretty Mrs. Adeney.

There was no chance that Madeleine would have the temerity to do so. Any idea she might have had in that direction had withered and died on their first meeting.

"Where did they find you?" Mrs. Adeney had demanded, her whole stance showing her immediate hostility to the younger girl.

Madeleine had stood there, tongue-tied, half suspecting that her own looks had something to do with Mrs. Adeney's question. She was small and dark, with a honey-coloured skin that gave her a truly peach like complexion. Large brown eyes, usually bright with laughter, were well placed beneath straight black eyebrows that mirrored the raven blackness of her hair. She was not to everyone's taste – Mrs. Adeney was much more the conventional beauty, with long, straight legs, blue-grey eyes, and the well-groomed look that Americans everywhere have made their own – but there was a spicy delight about the eager way she met life headlong that had an attraction of its own.

"I work here, in the office," she had said.

"Oh well," Mrs. Adeney had considered, "I suppose it could have been worse. How do you feel about being my Girl Friday for a while?"

Madeleine was placed in a quandary. She longed to see Istanbul for herself, but she had not immediately taken to Mrs. Adeney who was to make this possible.

6

"I shall do my best," she had said.

"Let's hope that is enough," Mrs. Adeney had countered. "It will be as long as you keep quiet and out of my way and don't get ideas that you've been elected to be my keeper to keep me on the straight and narrow. I expect you'll find it rather dull, but that won't be my fault. *I* didn't ask to have you along!"

The annoying thing was that Madeleine had found it rather dull. Ever since their arrival she had been stuck in the hotel in the new part of the city while her employer had made some half-hearted efforts to find her brother-in-law Mark who, she claimed, was somewhere in Istanbul, if he wasn't off enjoying himself with some woman. Madeleine had received the impression that Ursula Adeney's brother-in-law was a wolf who didn't have to bother with any sheep's clothing. If half the stories that Ursula told about him were true, he was everything that Madeleine most disliked, a man who used his wealth to bowl over innocent young women and who then boasted of his conquests to all and sundry. Madeleine secretly hoped that he would remain lost "somewhere in the country".

But today everything was different. Ursula had received an invitation from some fellow Americans who were living in Istanbul and had gone out happily with them for the afternoon, and Madeleine was busy rejoicing in her few hours of freedom. She had decided to spend the time sightseeing, an activity that Ursula hated, and had come first to the Topkapi Palace because it was a place that she had heard of and wanted to see for herself.

When she bought her ticket it was explained to her that she would need a further ticket if she wanted to see the Harem and she wandered across the courtyard to see the times when the various groups were allowed into what had once been the female quarters of the Ottoman Sultan's palace. By the time she had found the right place to buy this second ticket and had found out the time for the next English-speaking group, she had only ten minutes to spare and wandered over to where she could see the splendid view across the Bosphorus to the Asian part of the city. Some other people near her, who had a guide book with them, were pointing out the old Scutari hospital made famous by Florence Nightingale, and Madeleine looked at the huge building with interest, picturing in her mind how that indomitable lady must have found the place. Indeed, on the very spot where she stood, Suleiman the Magnificent had stood before her, and perhaps even the highly romanticised Roxelana, who had exercised such control over her lord and master, had seen this self-same view.

She returned to the Harem just as the doors were opening. She followed the others inside, taking a quick turn to the left into a small mosque, unadorned and without much interest. It was fun, she thought, to wonder what the other tourists were, what their nationality was and what they did. Some were easy enough to spot when it came to nationality; the slightly earnest, studious British couple hung about with guidebooks, the French couple who were equally determined not to be impressed, and some Americans who had just come from Athens and who were still there in spirit. Only one man defied being put into any category. He came in alone, his face sunburned and weathered, contrasting with his pale grey eyes. He was not French, though the beret he wore had made her think that he might be at first. He was certainly not British! She glanced at him again. He must be a Turk, she thought, and wondered what he was doing there, for there were no other Turks in the group.

He went straight to the front, pushing his way easily through the waiting people and peering at the *mihrab*, the decorated niche in the wall that points towards Mecca. He made his examination unhurriedly, unaware, or so it seemed, of the interest he was causing all round him. Then he straightened up, turned abruptly and walked to the back of the mosque, pausing just beside Madeleine. She pretended she had not been watching him, half turning her back on him, very much aware of the slight smile that he threw in her direction.

"Hullo, Melâhat!" he said out of the side of his mouth.

She looked straight ahead of her, not moving a muscle, turning his words over in her mind. She hadn't a clue as to what Melâhat could mean, but she thought his intention to be obvious. It was a temptation to turn her head a little and see how he was taking her dismissal of his approach, but she wouldn't allow herself to do so. Instead she could feel the colour surging up her cheeks as she realised that he had become aware of her tactics.

Happily for her peace of mind the guide began to collect up his party at that particular moment. He was a nervous young man, not very happy in either of the two languages he professed to speak.

"You are all English?" he asked hopefully.

Both the French and the Americans denied this. "But you speak English?" he said to the Americans. "I will say everything in both English and French. All right? We go!"

The stranger who had called Madeleine Melâhat ignored the guide. "We are only able to see a small part of the whole Harem," he told Madeleine. "The rest of it is still being restored. Besides, it is far too large. There are at least three hundred rooms in all. But it pays to have some idea of the basic plan of the building before you start. What do you know about the workings of the Harem?"

"Nothing," Madeleine admitted coolly.

"I thought not! You didn't even know this is a mosque, did you?"

Madeleine wished she had kept with the others even while they crowded out of the door. "I thought it might be," she said. "I want to hear what the guide has to say, so do you mind –?"

"You'll do far better with me," he insisted. "You have to understand the politics of the Harem if you are to appreciate the building properly. This is the mosque of the Black Eunuchs whose job it was to guard the women. There were White Eunuchs too, but their function was somewhat different, and anyway, the Black Eunuchs were considered to be more satisfactory in an all-female society. The Chief Black Eunich was called Kizlar Agasi, the Lord of the Girls, and he had a great deal of real power, being the most important official of the Harem. If you were one of the inmates it paid to keep in with him.''

Madeleine barely repressed a shudder. The corridor they were going down was gloomy and she couldn't help feeling sorry for the people who had been forced to live there. When they went into the Courtyard of the Black Eunuchs, she could only gasp with horror. The living quarters were arranged in three storeys round a small covered courtyard, with about ten tiny cells on each floor. Seeing that there were several hundred eunuchs, they must have slept in relays and in acute discomfort. The stranger pointed out some solid-looking sticks that were used for punishment by being applied to the soles of the feet.

"But it wasn't all bad," he went on, and she was conscious that he was fully aware of her distaste. "At least one of them was the real ruler of the whole Empire, no mean achievement in any age! And then there were the perks of the job. He could sell his urine as an aphrodisiac to the whole men who looked down on him and make a handsome profit on the deal, especially as he was obliged to pass water rather often –''

Madeleine felt that she had heard enough. She made a dive out of the courtyard and hurried after the rest of the group, losing herself amongst them as fast as she could. The guide pointed out the staircase that led to the Princes' Schoolrooms where the sons of the Sultan received their schooling, and then they were on the move again, hurrying through the courtyard where the women slaves were housed, and on to the apartments of the Valide Sultan, the rooms of the Sultan's mother, the most important woman in the Harem, who frequently acquired sufficient power to dominate her son and through him the whole Empire. The bedroom was particularly ornate, with tiled walls and painted ceiling.

"Would these have suited you?" Madeleine heard the stranger's voice ask. She turned on her heel, hoping that he wouldn't guess that she was at a loss as to how to get rid of him.

"Did Roxelana sleep here?" she asked the guide.

The young man blinked at her. "Roxelana?" he repeated. "I am not sure that she lived at this palace."

"She means Haseki Hürrem," the irrepressible stranger supplied. "And no, she didn't live here. The earliest date of any of these Harem buildings is during the reign of her grandson."

Madeleine watched fatalistically as most of the group detached themselves from the official guide and began to ply the stranger with questions as to how the women had actually lived in the Harem. "What a life!" they murmured at intervals.

"It was better than many others," he answered abruptly. "Many Western European women deliberately sold themselves into the Harem of the Sultan. Perhaps the alternatives weren't too grand at home!"

"But they must have been jealous of one another!"

The stranger smiled. "Women are frequently jealous, even today, wouldn't you agree?"

The guide gave up his attempt to reclaim his audience. He said something in Turkish to the stranger, who laughed. The guide smiled too and slapped the stranger on the back with a philosophical gesture. "Maruk Bey can tell you better than I!" he told the group.

So he was Turkish! Madeleine glanced at him covertly, taking a renewed interest in him. He wasn't particularly tall, she noticed, but he had an air of command that went well with his present surroundings. She could imagine his broad shoulders covered with silken cloth and embroidered in gold

11

and silver, with the stylised shapes of tulips, or one of the other preferred patterns of the sultans of old. Certainly she had never met a man like him before, and she wasn't quite sure that she liked him at all. He was so aggressively masculine and she didn't like being made so vividly conscious of anyone. Even when she didn't look at him she could feel him there, his presence sending prickles up her spine in a way that she definitely did not like.

She turned her head and saw that he was watching her too and that he didn't feel any need to look away when their eyes met. On the contrary, he seemed to be waiting for her to say something. She coloured and bit her lip.

"I was saying," he said, "that an ambitious girl would take care to stay on the right side of the Valide Sultan. Her son would come and take coffee, or tea, with his mother, and it was a good time for a pretty girl to catch his eye. If she were successful, the Sultan would signify his wishes to his mother and the girl would be dressed in all the finery that the women could manage. She would then be known as *gözde*, 'in the eye'."

His mocking glance fell on Madeleine and he half-winked at her. She would not make the mistake of looking at him again, she promised herself. Why, he was deliberately *flirting* with her! That was bad enough in itself, but she could see from the amused glances of everyone around her that they had all noticed and were enjoying the silent exchange – only it wasn't an exchange exactly, because she couldn't see that she had done anything at all to encourage him.

"If she gave her lord great pleasure," Maruk Bey went on, the slight smile on his face deepening and his eyes still on Madeleine's face, "she might become one of his favourites. Their number varied from time to time, but there were usually twelve of them, known as *ikbal*, which means in Turkish success or good fortune. There was only one better thing to be, and that was to be the mother of a male child, a *kadin*, a potential Valide Sultan, in fact." He bowed slightly in Madeleine's direction. "Shall we go on to the Sultan's apartments?" he asked the company at large.

Madeleine went through the remaining rooms in a whirl. Afterwards all she could remember of them were their magnificent decorations, all done, according to Maruk Bey, by the great architect Sinan, in whom he had a particular interest. She remembered wondering if the slapping water of the fountain had gone on all night, and comparing the sultan's bath with that of Queen Victoria at Osborne, and being delighted with the room where the little princes had met for recreation, where the beauty of the stained glass windows, set at an angle in the plaster, seemed particularly vivid. She remembered too being told that the Court of the Favourites had also been known as the House of Felicity and wondering if they had found happiness in their strange life.

Then, suddenly, they were back almost at the place where they had started the tour and the doors clanged to release them into another part of the palace. Madeleine stepped out into the sunshine, giving her shoulders a shake to cast off the last of the Council Place of the Jinns below the princes' dormitory, all of them, she was convinced, in league with Maruk Bey, for how else could he have made her so aware of his every gesture as he had rehearsed the plotting that had gone on there in the past and the spectacular cruelty of some of the sultans, one of whom had thrown every woman in the Harem into the Bosphorus to drown because he was tired of the lot of them. He hadn't given any sign of disapproval, Madeleine remembered indignantly. He had just told them the story as though it had been the obvious thing to do! How glad she was to leave him behind and return to the modern world —

"Well, Melâhat, did you enjoy your tour?"

She stopped short, bitterly aware that her heart was beating faster at the sound of his voice, and resenting the fact as much as she resented him.

"I should have preferred to have heard the official guide,"

she responded coolly. "His account might not have been as full as yours, but I'm sure it would have been more agreeable."

He put a hand easily on her arm and led her through the palace gardens. "How little you know yourself. Your vivid imagination was on fire with the possibilities of harem life. Did you cast yourself as an immediate favourite, or as the Valide Sultan herself?" He shook his head at her, deliberately mocking her. "You are too young for that quite yet. I think you would have to start as *gözde* on your very first day there! That is much more possible!"

"I didn't think about it." She pulled her arm away from him and rubbed her elbow thoughtfully. "Though I'm sure you had yourself cast as Sultan!"

"But of course," he agreed immediately. "With you inside the Harem, what other role could I possibly have?"

A stifled gasp escaped her lips. "Will you please leave me alone?" she demanded.

"If you really want me to. I thought you might like to see the porcelain collection in the palace kitchens. It is world-famous, you know. It would be a pity to miss it because you were determined to be coy."

It was the last word that did it! If there was something she was not it was *coy*! She had never been coy in her life!

"How dare you?" She positively seethed with temper. "Please go away! Now!"

But he ignored her annoyance. The now familiar mocking smile darted across his face. "You will be quite safe in my company," he told her. "At least for today! All right?"

She didn't know why she should, but she believed him and, if she were safe to retire from the fray when she pleased, she couldn't help knowing that she would find the porcelain collection and everything else a great deal more exciting in his presence. Perhaps it was because he was Turkish that he was different from any other man who had come her way? She had never met a Turk before, but they were bound to be different from the Occidental males whom she mixed with at home, and that was exciting too, in its own way.

"All right," she agreed, and smiled at him, wondering at herself a little. Then a new fear came to her. Supposing now that she had given way he found her boring, or lacking in the feminine appeal he obviously expected the women of his acquaintance to have? Or, worse still, supposing he should be shocked by her ignorance of his customs and way of life? She couldn't believe it was anything like the more ordinary life she lived at home. She licked her lips nervously. "But I have my own ticket!" she added quickly.

His chuckle unnerved her. It was unkind of him to underline the fragility of her defences against him. She sought vainly for something to say that would put him in his place once and for all, but once again he was before her.

"I've told you that you are safe with me," he reminded her. "Why don't you throw that uncomfortable discretion of yours to the winds, because I'm not going to let you go?"

"But you must! I have to get back to the hotel. My employer will start enquiries if I don't get back when I said I would!"

"And when is that?"

She looked at him suspiciously, but he was no longer laughing at her. "After tea," she admitted.

"Then you have plenty of time to see the porcelain and to have tea with me," he said with decision. "We can leave the treasury for another day."

Madeleine followed him meekly past an exotic-looking throne, back into the main courtyard that was planted with trees and flowers and cobbled pathways that traversed it from one side to the other. Maruk Bey held out his hand to her and, when she placed hers a little cautiously in his, he smiled at her, his pale grey eyes praising her so obviously that she blushed.

"You should pay attention to these gardens," he told her.

"It was from here that the tulip was taken to Holland."

"Istanbul was very important, wasn't it?" she said awkwardly.

"Very," he agreed. "It was the main crossroads of the world. Geography has a great deal to do with history. It was inescapable that Istanbul should grow great on trade and conquest and that later the sheer size of her empire should hold the seeds of her downfall, as with Byzantine Constantinople before her."

Madeleine creased her brow in an effort to remember what she knew about either period of history. "Where did the Turks come from?" she asked. "Surely the Byzantines spoke Greek?"

"They came from central Europe, from where Turkestan is today, where they speak a much purer kind of Turkish than is spoken in modern Turkey today. A great wave of people came flooding into Europe. The Turks stopped here, others stopped on the great plains of Hungary, and yet others made their way up to Finland. All three languages are closely related and are quite different from the Indo-European languages that are spoken by the rest of Europe – except the Basques."

"Then the Hungarians and the Finns came from Asia at one time?"

"We all came from somewhere else at one time." He looked teasingly at her. "Even the English!"

The porcelain was so beautiful that Madeleine ran out of exclamations. She had seen the occasional Ming vase before in museums, but she had never seen them in such lavish quantities as these dinner services, bowls, and water jars. Wonderful celadons of the Sung and Yuan dynasties made the Chinese collection the greatest outside Peking and made the European collection of French and German china seem dull by comparison.

"Thank you very much for showing me that!" she said as they made their way out of the kitchens again. "It's been a

16

lovely afternoon!"

His eyes glinted strangely. "It has, hasn't it? Are you ready for tea, Melâhat?"

She made no protest at all when he walked her out of the main gates and found a taxi, instructing it to take them to the Galata Tower. "I think you'll like it," he said, getting in beside her. "The views of the Bosphorus and the Golden Horn are particularly good from the top."

He was right, as she was beginning to think he always was. They sat at a table on the top of the ancient Genoese tower and watched the sunset light up the skyline of old Stamboul, the slender, pencil-thin minarets of the many mosques etched out against the orange and scarlet sky.

"Istanbul never disappoints," he said. "You see, it is quite as romantic as you thought it would be, isn't it?"

She nodded, hoping that he didn't know that some of the romance she felt was because he was sitting beside her. "This is the first time I've been able to see anything of it," she confided. "My – my employer doesn't care for sightseeing. She's here to look for her brother-in-law."

"Why? Is he lost?" Maruk Bey drawled lazily, his grey eyes losing their customary amused look.

"He sounds awful to me!" Madeleine burst out. "He's a ladies' man of the worst type and at present he's away with some woman in the country. He's supposed to be lecturing at the University of the Bosphorus, but he doesn't seem to take even that very seriously –"

"You know him well?" Maruk Bey cut across her.

Madeleine hesitated. "No," she admitted. "But he must be awful, because he boasts of his conquests to his family. I hate men who kiss and tell!"

"A heinous crime," he agreed lightly. "But perhaps it is your employer who has an inventive turn of mind?"

Madeleine considered this. "Perhaps. But I don't think so. Why should she make up things about him? She likes him very much. In fact that's why she's here. She wants him to go back to the States and help her with her company. Her husband was killed in Viet-Nam, you see, and she needs help, but this man won't even see her!''

Maruk Bey's smile hardened into a mask that frightened her, it was so unyielding. She wished she hadn't mentioned Ursula Adeney, but had kept to the safer topic of the city of Istanbul.

"How do you know he won't see your employer?" he asked.

"He's away, and he hasn't left any address. I think he knew she was coming and is determined to avoid her —''

"And you blame him for that?"

Madeleine had the uncomfortable feeling that he was setting great store on her answer and she could feel her cheeks growing hot as she tried to sort out exactly what she did think about the Adeneys.

"No," she said at last. "I don't blame him. Ursula Adeney isn't very easy always. She's beautiful and far too young to be a widow. I think he ought to help her with her business, Adeney Publications, if he's as clever as she says he is, but I can understand his not wanting to."

Maruk Bey said nothing. He glanced restlessly at his watch and signalled to the waiter for the bill, paying it with a few coins from his pocket. Madeleine regarded him miserably. It had been just as she had feared, he was bored with her and wanted to be gone as quickly as possible!

"Must we go already?" she asked.

"'Fraid so. Come on, Melâhat, I'll put you in a taxi that will take you back to your hotel."

She picked up her handbag and her gloves, determined not to show him that his dismissal had hurt her. "I don't usually work for Mrs. Adeney," she said, her mouth trembling a little. "I work in the London office of Adeney Publications. I'm very grateful to her for bringing me here!"

His expression softened for a fleeting instant. "Never mind,

18

Melâhat, there will be other adventures for you." He touched her cheek and she winced away from him as if he had burnt her.

"I don't look for adventures!" she denied haughtily. "And I can see myself into a taxi."

"Just as you like." It seemed that he could be every bit as haughty as she. All the way down in the lift she hoped for some sign that he would unbend and make a move to see her again, but he appeared to have forgotten all about her already. "You can get a taxi over there," he told her, pointing down the street towards a small square.

She started down the street, but she couldn't leave him without a word, even if he were prepared to do just that. She turned back uncertainly. "Thank you for telling me about the Harem and – everything," she said stiffly.

The mocking smile lit his eyes as he sketched her a salute. "Be good, Melâhat. Perhaps I shall see you in London one day."

"Oh yes!" she exclaimed. "And then I can show you every-thing!" But he had already turned away and was walking away from her in the opposite direction and her eagerness died with every step he took. If he did come to London, he wouldn't know where to find her, and he quite clearly didn't want to anyway. She gave herself a mental shake and stepped out briskly down the street. It made no difference to her! He could do as he liked! How could someone she had only just met that afternoon have effect on her? She stepped into the first taxi and gave the driver the name of her hotel, pretending to herself that she was interested in every detail of the streets that they hurried up and down.

She had liked Maruk Bey, though. She had more than liked him. She had found the way he looked at her deliciously ex-citing, even while it had embarrassed her. She would have liked to have seen him again, to explore a new knowledge of herself that only he had ever given her cause to suspect was there. In fact she was more bitterly disappointed than she could remember being since as a child she had been denied some long-awaited treat. The streets passed her by in a blur, and she was horrified to discover that the blur was caused by her own tears, so she sat up very straight and made a great play of recognising the street where her hotel was and over-tipped the driver with outrageous abandon, and felt more sorry for herself then she ever had. But, as she couldn't stand on the pavement for ever, she sniffed back her tears and walked deliberately into the lighted hotel, her head held high.

CHAPTER II

MADELEINE went straight to the reception desk to collect the key of her room. "But, madame," the uniformed man behind the counter gasped, "you have already checked out. Madame Adeney and yourself are flying to Ankara. Why are you not with her?"

Madeleine felt as confused as he looked. "You must have made some mistake," she managed to say. "Mrs. Adeney spent the day with friends."

The man nodded. "But she came back soon after lunch, much excited, and paid her bill. She took everything with her, mademoiselle – your own luggage as well as her own!"

A prickle of cold lodged itself somewhere in Madeleine's throat. "But she can't have done!"

"You ought to be with her!" the man insisted. "She has your passport with her, as well as your suitcase, and we have let your room to another person!"

Madeleine swallowed hard. She must not panic, she told herself. There had to be a logical, reasonable explanation! Ursula Adeney would be the last person to leave another person stranded, alone, in a foreign city. Madeleine conjured up a picture of the American girl with her wilful twist to the lips and the hard, unhappy expression behind her eyes, and began to wonder. *But she wouldn't do a thing like this!* Would she?

"Perhaps I should see the manager," she said aloud. "Mrs. Adeney must have left some address for me to contact–"

"*Yes*, mademoiselle!" the man exclaimed in relief. "I will fetch the manager immediately!"

But the manager was a long time coming. Madeleine found herself a seat beside the display of postcards and spent an anxious few minutes trying to persuade herself that the whole thing was a mistake. But as the evening wore on, she began to wish that she could at least have changed her clothes. Her sailcloth trousers had seemed bright and in tune with her mood when she had gone out, but the only people in the foyer now had all changed for the evening and she felt increasingly out of place. Indeed, after a while she began to imagine that they were all looking enquiringly at her, and she wished heartily that the manager would hurry up and come.

When the manager did finally come he looked as distraught as she felt.

"I am sorry to have kept you waiting," he began, wringing his hands with deep feeling. "This is a terrible situation! Terrible! Such a thing has never happened in my hotel before!"

"Quite!" Madeleine cut him off. "The sooner we get in contact with Mrs. Adeney the better for both of us. What address did she leave?"

"She didn't!" the manager said baldly. "That is what I have been doing, making enquiries of all my staff. I could not believe it to be possible that she would vanish – pouff – leaving you here! What does she expect *us* to do? It is incomprehensible! Not even your passport has been left here!"

Madeleine gave in to the weakness of her knees and sat down again. "This is ridiculous!" she declared.

"We must fetch the police," the manager began again. "They must take charge of you. One thing is certain, you cannot remain here without money or passport –"

"Or clothes!" Madeleine chimed in.

"Madame Adeney must have been mad! What did she expect you to do? I am very sorry, mademoiselle, but you realise that it is impossible for you to stay here!"

"If you say so," Madeleine said wearily. "But must it be the police?"

22

"What other solution is there? They will be able to check where she is staying in Ankara – if in fact that is where she has gone. I can do *nothing*! I am not responsible for this catastrophe! I must protect the hotel –"

"But there must be some way of finding Mrs. Adeney –"

"Then tell me how, mademoiselle? Me, I am not omniscient! How do I find out where she is, tell me that!"

Madeleine winced. "You could have found out where she was going!"

"And why should I do that? How could I know that you were not with the lady as she implied?" He wrung his hands more furiously than ever. "That such a thing should happen in my hotel!" A thought struck him and he looked speculatively down at Madeleine. "Perhaps you know someone else in Istanbul?" he asked.

Madeleine shook her head. The full significance of her situation was beginning to come home to her. But *the police*! There must be some other way.

"Mrs. Adeney has a brother-in-law in Istanbul –"

The manager flashed a relieved smile. "Then you have only to tell me his address and I shall telephone him at once!"

"Yes," Madeleine agreed. There was a pause while she reflected on the best way of presenting her bad news. "I don't know his address. Mrs. Adeney was here to look for him." She raised her eyes fleetingly and looked away again hastily at the manager's frosty expression. "Mrs. Adeney thought he might have gone into the country on – on holiday."

"I see. Do you know where this Mr. Adeney works? The American Consulate? Something like that?"

Madeleine gave a little gasp of triumph. "He lectures at the University!" she exclaimed. "Oh, please, will you find out from them where he lives?"

The manager nodded enthusiastically. "The University is on holiday, but I will enquire. You have no need to worry further, mademoiselle. Someone in the University will know."

Madeleine chewed her lip anxiously. "Mrs. Adeney said it was the University of the Bosphorus –"

"I will make enquiries at once!" the manager purred.

Even so, he was gone for a long time and Madeleine had more than enough time to imagine that he could get no answer. She was beginning to wonder what the police cells of Istanbul were like when he came back in triumph, his face wreathed in smiles.

"All is well, mademoiselle! I have the address in my hand. They were very reluctant to present me with it because strict instructions had been left that Mr. Adeney's address was to be given to no one, but when they heard of your plight they were naturally eager to help. It is possible that Mrs. Adeney was right and Mr. Adeney is on holiday, but they are sure there will be no difficulty about your staying in his house until Mrs. Adeney can be found in Ankara."

Madeleine thanked him, for, in his own way, he had tried to be kind, much embarrassed as he had been by her presence. She accepted the address he had written down on a piece of paper for her, and tried not to mind too much when he hurried her out into the dark of the night where the wind struck cold against her bare arms, making her shiver.

She had been astonished to discover that Mr. Adeney lived on the Asian side of the city. The manager, between thrusting her out of the door and waving her on her way, had told her that she would find the ferry down by the Galata Bridge and that it would cost her only a few pence to go on board. "The ferry to Üsküdar!" he called after her. "You will find it easily, very easily!"

She might have done if she had been able to understand one word of Turkish, but she couldn't. The language had no roots in common with her own and although some people spoke English they couldn't make out from her pronunciation where she wanted to go.

24

It was further to the bridge than she had imagined. The road led sharply downhill and the traffic was impossible. Cars whirled from one side of the road to the other, keeping up a constant obbligato of sound as the drivers spoke to one another by playing warnings on their horns of their next oncoming rush. But the Galata Bridge eventually came in sight, the first of the two that crossed the Golden Horn and joined the two European parts of the city together, the old and the new.

"Üsküdar?" Madeleine asked a rain-coated man hopefully.

He gave her a curious glance. "Üsküdar?" he repeated. He pointed across the bridge, shaking his head at her bare arms and the shiver of cold she was only barely repressing.

Madeleine hurried away from him, suddenly afraid of his interest. She felt very much alone and furiously angry with Ursula Adeney for having put her in this position. But her anger burned itself out in the face of her interest in her surroundings. There was so much going on all round the bridge. Fish stalls abounded, competing with others selling smooth, shiny rounds of bread, and yet others who were selling roasted chestnuts, or whole meals, to the passers-by. Ferry boats came and went on both sides of the bridge. On the Marmara Sea side, they were busy plying the Bosphorus; on the inland side, they came and went up the Golden Horn, bobbing round the larger ships that could only gain entry when the bridge was opened in the early hours of the morning.

It was tempting to stand in the middle of the bridge for a moment and see the reflection of the crescent moon shining out of the water below. It was a fitting symbol for the city, Madeleine thought, for in a way Istanbul had been the centre of the Islamic world for centuries. She thought that it had become a part of the Turkish flag, and of so many other Islamic nations, because once when the Franks had hoped to take the city under cover of darkness the brand new sickle moon had shone on the metal of their arms, giving away their positions, and the city had been saved. It looked well now competing with the stars over the slender minarets of the mosques of Old Stamboul.

The cold wind forbade lingering for long, however. Madeleine joined the hurrying footsteps of the crowds as they rushed homeward, hugging her handbag close to her, partly to give herself an illusion of warmth, and partly because she was afraid of losing it too like she had everything else. A gust of wind spattered some rain in her face and made her break into a run across the last few yards of the bridge. But then where? She had no idea which way to go. She asked at the first jetty and was pointed on to the next and then further on again. Then, at last, her money was accepted and she found herself in the midst of a jostling queue that was making its way forward across one tied-up ferry to another beyond.

Madeleine would have liked to have gone inside, but all the places were taken and she was forced to remain up on deck, staring out into the blackness of the Marmara Sea where it narrowed into the neck of the Bosphorus that joined it to the Black Sea a few miles further north. It was bitterly cold. Madeleine rubbed her bare arms with her hands, hoping to restore her circulation to something like its normal condition. Several pairs of sympathetic feminine eyes snapped at her from under folded headscarves that presumably gave the wearer the feeling that she was modestly dressed even if she did no longer wear the veil.

"Üsküdar," they whispered to her, and prodded her, pointing across the ship to the jetty they had just banged into with some force.

Madeleine thanked them in English, hopefully holding out the address she had been given, but the women only shook their heads and giggled, leaving Madeleine to suppose that they were none of them able to read.

Standing on the street, drops of waspish rain stinging her flesh, she thought she had never been more miserable. It was queer that one always thought of "abroad" as being permanently warm and bathed in sunshine. Istanbul, with winter rapidly closing in all over the northern hemisphere, was neither of these things.

"You want guide? You American?"

Madeleine turned in relief to face the plucking fingers of the dark-eyed boy who had accosted her.

"Oh yes! Though I'm English, actually." In that moment it couldn't have mattered less to her what she was, but habit made her plunge into further explanations. "I'm looking for the house of an American." She held out the address the hotel manager had given her. "Will you take me there?"

The boy nodded, glancing at the writing with an expression of contempt that grew into a delighted smile. "I take you now!" he announced, as though the writing spelt out some great treat to him. "Come now!"

Madeleine was only too willing. She followed where he led up a sloping street that ran along the edge of the Bosphorus. They went past a small hospital, an oasis of light that lit up the branches of a tree weighed down with sleeping birds. The boy pointed through a gap in the houses to the lights of Europe, made more romantic by the silent, gliding shapes of the ships that moved through the strange currents between the two continents.

"This is your house," the boy told her.

The house lay beneath the road, shining white with fresh paint in the light of the scescent moon. It was in complete darkness. The boy's disappointment at finding the place deserted matched her own. He raced down the steps to the front door, beating a tattoo on the knocker. Madeleine felt her way behind him, tears of desolation blinding her as she struggled for a footing on steps she couldn't see.

"I must get in!" she almost shouted.

The boy turned and looked at her. He jabbered at length, telling her something that she was too tired even to try and understand. At last he patted her kindly on the shoulder and signalled for her to wait for his return. She did so because she had no choice, bitterly aware of the scalding tears that trickled down her cheeks, the only warm thing left in this frozen world.

She could hear the boy shouting a greeting across the street above her. He was answered by the nasal tones of some women and, shortly afterwards, a woman's shadow blotted out the moon and someone came, protesting, down the steps towards Madeleine. The Turkish woman took out a key and unlocked the door, pushing her way into the house.

"Mihrimah!" the boy whispered to her.

Madeleine opened her purse and searched for a suitable coin to give him, amused by his eager interest in his expected tip. A caustic murmur from the Turkish woman made him give her a push towards the door and the light from the hall within. Madeleine's fingers closed round the largest coin she could find and she handed it to him, a little embarrassed by his effusive gratitude. When she turned away from him, she saw that the Turkish woman was studying her thoughtfully, and she stepped hastily into the house, hoping that she looked less of a mess than she felt.

"Is this Mr. Adeney's house?" she asked, slowly and clearly.

The Turkish woman nodded. She put out a large, capable hand and pulled Madeleine further into the hall, shutting the door firmly behind her. She pointed to herself. "Mihrimar," she said gruffly.

Madeleine attempted a smile. "Madeleine Carvill," she responded.

The woman jerked her head in approval. "Madeleine Hanim." Her face broke into a dazzling smile and she laughed, pantomiming a shiver to show that she knew how cold it was. With a commanding gesture she walked through the house, snapping on the lights as she went. She showed no surprise that a strange woman should call at her employer's house, but then, if Ursula was to be believed, she was probably accustomed to it. Madeleine, following the maid into the sitting room, began to hope that the absent Mr. Adeney would stay away, at least

28

until she was in better control of herself.

In the kitchen the maid thrust open the refrigerator to show the ample supplies inside and made a comprehensive gesture in the direction of the dining room. Madeleine peered round the door and was struck dumb by the beautiful sheen on the polished table and the shining silver of the candlesticks. The curtains fell to the floor, drawn back to reveal the lights of the city twinkling across the Bosphorus. When a ship came past, bearing the hammer and sickle of the U.S.S.R., it had the effect of looking as though it would come right into the room. Madeleine thought she had never been inside a finer house than this one.

Mihrimah came and stood beside her, touching her gently on the shoulder. Madeleine started and followed her obediently up the stairs, her embarrassment increasing as the maid pointed out the bathroom and the first of the bedrooms, where she clearly expected Madeleine to spend the night. Madeleine would have liked to have asked her what there was up the further flight of stairs, but Mihrimah had already turned her back on her and was ploughing down the stairs again, her heavy, thick-set body determined on its course. Madeleine followed more slowly. She was aware that the wide, marble staircase meant money, even if the furniture had been cheap and dreary. But as the furniture was, on the contrary, beautifully chosen and most of it antique; it more than matched the graceful lines of the house. And therein lay the worry. How did Mr. Adeney afford to live in such a house? This was not the sort of setting she would have expected a university lecturer to have chosen for himself, so how could he afford it?

This gnawing anxiety remained with her long after Mihrimah had departed. She went to the door with the Turkish woman, holding the front door wide open so that the light from the hall would shine on to the steps.

"Goodnight," she called after her, and immediately felt foolish, for the other woman clearly didn't understand her.

"Gülegüle!" Mihrimah answered her with a final laugh. She had obviously never met anyone anything like Madeleine before.

The house seemed very empty when she had gone. Madeleine pattered round the downstairs rooms trying to make herself feel at home. She wasn't at all successful. She stood in the middle of the kitchen for a long time half-heartedly telling herself that the unknown Mr. Adeney wouldn't mind if she got herself something to eat. It was a long time since the disastrous tea she had shared with Maruk Bey at the top of the Galata Tower and she was beginning to think that the peculiar sensation in her stomach was not nerves as she had first thought, but sheer animal hunger.

As time went on her confidence returned and she began to feel quite gay. It was obvious that Mr. Adeney was still away and that she would have the house to herself all night. This was such a pleasant prospect that she began to cook herself a meal with something like her normal zest. There was rice which she put on to boil, and some of the most luscious-sized carrots she had ever seen. The meat was more of a problem, but she soon discovered some shish-kebab swords on which she skewered anything she could find in the fridge. It turned out to be a delicious meal which she ate in the kitchen, carefully removing all traces of the feast afterwards. It was still possible that the unknown Mr. Adeney would be displeased if he found she had made herself too much at home.

Such a consideration did not dissuade her from going into the sitting room, however. She drew up a chair beside the window and sat there in the dark, trying to imagine what the scene would be like in daylight. When she tired of that, she turned on the light and prowled round the room trying to discover clues as to what Mr. Adeney would be like.

A single glance at the bookshelves told her that he had little in common with his sister-in-law. True, there was a stack of Adeney Publications* magazines, but they had hardly been opened, unlike the books that stood cheek by jowl with them, books on every topic under the sun in both English and Turkish. Ursula would have read the magazines and left the architectural tracts and the rather heavy history books severely alone.

From the books, Madeleine's gaze fell on the carpet. She knew by the look of it that it was a beautiful example of the Turkish art, but she was in no position to judge its value. She was content to make out the stylised pattern and to wonder how old it was and if it were hand-made.

A glance at her watch told her that it was nearly eleven o'clock and she longed for bed. The thought of sleep drew her like a magnet back up the stairs and into the bedroom. She had no reason to suppose that anyone else was going to sleep there. The sheets on the bed were freshly laundered and there was no sign of any pyjamas, such as Mr. Adeney would surely wear.

Madeleine opened the wardrobe and ran her eye over the contents. A very masculine set of clothing met her glance, the trousers neatly hung beside their jackets, and the shirts and underclothes stacked in neat piles in the drawers at one side. There were no pyjamas! The nearest approach she could find to nightclothes was a thigh-length robe of Chinese silk that glimmered from green to gold in the discreet electric lighting. She would have a bath, she decided, and then she would go to bed in his robe, and he could just like it or lump it!

She was about to close the door of the wardrobe again when she caught sight of a very feminine-looking piece of apparel lying on the floor of the wardrobe. She pulled it out and held it up, a little shocked by its brevity. The brassiere was one of the least modest she had seen and, though the skirt was long, it was attached to a very scanty pair of pants, designed to reveal far more than they were meant to hide.

"Goodness!" Madeleine exclaimed aloud.

She hid the costume again on the floor of the wardrobe, but not before she had decided that the skirts were too long for

31

her even while the rest of it might have fitted her very well. If she had the courage to wear such a garment. If courage was what was needed! It was the brazenest, most immodest dress she had ever seen, even for a belly-dancer to wear, and it had quite obviously been made for a belly-dancer. Perhaps they grew used to appearing little better than stark naked in public! She thought she could imagine the kind of girl who would wear it; what it was doing in Mr. Adeney's wardrobe required no imagination whatsoever!

Madeleine ran her bath in the full flurry of self-righteousness her find had aroused in her. If anything had been needed to confirm Ursula Adeney's judgement on her brother-in-law, that had been it. Why, if she went upstairs to the other bedrooms, what would she find up there? She wouldn't think about it! With any luck, she would have found Ursula and be out of that house long before its lady-killing owner came home from his "trip to the country"!

Lying in the bath with the hot water dissipating much of her disquiet, Madeleine was forced to admit that she did share her host's taste for luxury, whatever she thought of his morals. The hot water was truly hot, the bath was solid marble and shaped to receive the human body in comfort, and the towels were dry, warm and simply enormous. She wasn't quite so sure that she approved of the mirrors that covered the greater part of walls, but once she got used to seeing herself looking back at her from all sides, she found she didn't dislike it as much as she felt she ought. The trouble was, she told herself sternly, she was as vain as he was. She even *liked* looking at herself!

She thought she looked undeniably attractive in Mr. Adeney's dressing-gown. It reached far lower than her thighs, of course, coming well down to her knees, and it was far too big across the shoulders, but the glow of the silk reflected the glow of her newly bathed skin in the most pleasing fashion. As a garment, she thought that it was wasted on a man. She wished that she had anything in her own wardrobe that was half as nice!

The bed was of course a double one, an unaccustomed luxury when one was used to sleeping in a two-foot-six bed in one's parents' house. Madeleine tried not to dwell on the usual occupant of the bed, and this was easier than it might have been, for she fell fast asleep as soon as her head touched the pillow. It was like falling into a comfortable, feather-bedded darkness from which she never wanted to awaken.

But awaken she did! For an instant she couldn't remember where she was and the noise she could hear meant nothing to her. She sat up sharply and listened intently. It was a very female noise. Yes, there it was again! A yelp of pleasure followed by a giggle. It was exactly as she had expected – Mr. Adeney was home!

But then the noises changed. The female laughter changed to pleas which were finally silenced. Madeleine had a horrid fear that she ought to march downstairs and do what she could to rescue the unfortunate girl who had fallen into Mr. Adeney's clutches. Honesty, however, forced her to admit that it was extremely unlikely that the girl would welcome being rescued, especially now that she was giggling again, her soft, high voice echoing cheerfully round the house.

Madeleine wished heartily that she hadn't awoken, for what was she to do? She couldn't go downstairs and interrupt – whatever there was to interrupt, and yet she could hardly go on sitting in his bed when he showed every sign of needing it at any moment. She could imagine his fury when he discovered her there, uninvited and unannounced, and she felt a tremble of genuine fear that he would send her packing there and then.

Actually, he sounded rather nice. She could hear his deep voice answering the girl's, even while she couldn't understand what he said. His Turkish was as fluent as her own was nonexistent!

"*Ne istyor sunuz?*" The words came sharply, quite different from the lazy tones he had spoken to the laughing girl. Madeleine strained her ears to hear what was going on and immediately she recognised the nasal tones of Mihrimah.

"What?" the man exclaimed in English, and then the sound of his laughter filled the house. "Is she, though?"

That had torn it, Madeleine reflected. Mihrimah had obviously told him about her own unwanted presence. She was surprised that he didn't sound angrier, but all she could hear was his laughter and the sharp, reproving whine of the girl, begging for she knew not what.

Mihrimah spoke again in amused enquiry. The man gave his consent and the front door opened and closed with a bang. This was followed by an outraged wail and a long silence. Madeleine clenched her fists and made a movement to get out of bed, but she was too late. The girl had gone and the man's footsteps tapped lightly on the marble stairs as he ran lightly up them.

Frozen to the spot, she saw his shadow appear in the doorway. He was not as tall as she had imagined he would be. Somehow she had thought he would be much taller than Ursula with her long-legged grace, but he was scarcely as tall as his sister-in-law. Indeed, he was much the same size and shape as her Turkish escort of the afternoon. The thought of Maruk Bey set her heart pounding, and she made to turn on the light, changed her mind, and hugged her knees against her chest instead.

The man snapped on the overhead light and they stared at one another. He was leaning, very much at his leisure, against the jamb of the door, and he was smiling. Madeleine's jaw dropped and she swallowed the lump in her throat. *She was in the wrong house!* This was never Ursula Adeney's brother-in-law! It couldn't be!

"Maruk Bey!" she whispered.

He bowed his head, his eyes looking with interest at his dressing-gown. She blushed and pulled it higher up around her throat, tightening the belt so hard that it almost cut her in two.

"I – I hope you don't mind?" she went on tentatively.

His smile deepened. "Well, well," he said. "Melâhat Hanim!"

She sank back against the pillows, annoyed that her deepening colour must surely tell him how his presence disturbed her.

"I found it in your wardrobe," she said. "The other – dress didn't fit!"

He moved his head slightly. "That is a pity, though you look quite fetching in my robe. Have you no clothes of your own that you must rob my closet for something to wear?"

"My clothes were wet," she explained.

"I'm not complaining," he drawled. His light grey eyes shone brilliantly as he gazed at her. "Melâhat," he said deliberately.

"I'll go!" she said.

He ignored that. "How did you find my *yali*?" he asked.

She stole a look at him. "I don't know what a *yali* is." How could he stand there like that, not moving a muscle and reducing her to *pulp*?

"A *yali* is a villa that fronts the waterside," he explained.

"Oh," she said. Her eyes met his and she blushed vividly. "I don't know what Melâhat means either," she complained.

He moved his shoulders against the doorway. "Melâhat is the Turkish for beauty," he drawled. "I find you very beautiful."

Madeleine's mouth felt suddenly dry and she pulled the bedclothes closer about her in a defensive movement that brought the laughter into his grey eyes.

"Dark, mysterious, and very, very beautiful!" he said.

CHAPTER III

NOBODY had ever called Madeleine beautiful to her face before. She turned the compliment over in her mind while the silence grew between them and threatened to overwhelm her. *Beautiful!* Imagine someone like Maruk Bey thinking her beautiful! But perhaps it was just a figure of speech? Worse still, perhaps he had told the girl downstairs, and who knew how many others, that she was beautiful too? She thought it only too likely.

"How did you find my house?" he asked her again.

The negligent attitude of his body did nothing to conceal his strength or the hard masculinity that was so much a part of him. It was impossible not to be conscious of the brilliant look in his eyes, just as it was impossible not to react to it by the growing gust of excitement within her.

"I came to the wrong house," she said.

His eyebrows arched in enquiry. "On the contrary, this is very much the right house!" A small smile played on his lips as he eased himself upright and came across the room towards her. "Did you follow me home this afternoon?"

She shook her head, watching him warily. He sat down on the bed beside her and she wriggled away from him hastily.

"Frightened, Melâhat? You have no need to be!"

She thought she had every need to be frightened of him. She licked her lips in unconscious appeal and sought for the right words to fend him off. Close to, he was an even more devastating proposition, and she had no idea how she was going to handle the situation.

He touched her cheek with light fingers, following the trail of colour that fled up her cheeks.

36

"I thought this was Mr. Adeney's house," she whispered.

His hand checked for a minute before tracing the line of her jaw and resting on the collar of the gown she was wearing. Then he pulled her irresistibly towards him, taking a firm grip of the silken cloth, the light in his eyes turning to a blazing fire. "Please!" she murmured, but he paid no attention to her plea. He bent his head and his lips claimed hers with a force that staggered her. There was no gentleness in the caress, not even the support of his arms, only the demanding hardness of lips that commanded her surrender.

"Has no one ever taught you to kiss before?" he asked, releasing his grip on her collar and fingering the nape of her neck instead.

"No," Madeleine said. "And you're not going to either!"

His laughter answered her and his lips reclaimed hers, forcing her back against the pillows. The harsh urgency of his kiss evoked a bewildering response within her. His attitude was that of master, and she was ashamed to discover that she liked it, but she couldn't allow him to have his way. It might not occur to him to consult her, or to care whether she was a willing partner or not, but it mattered to her. She had her own standards to live by. She pulled herself free with a sobbing gasp and fled to the other side of the bed, standing on knees that threatened to give way beneath her.

"I won't!" she exclaimed.

He rolled over, eyeing her with mockery. "Then why come here?" he asked.

"Not for *that*! I came to find Mr. Adeney. Mark Adeney! I was told this was his house. How was I to know that you lived here? Or that you – that you – You shouldn't have sent your *friend* away!"

His eyes seemed to look straight through the dressing-gown she was wearing and she clutched at its gaping front with agitated hands, blushing fiercely.

"Of course I sent her away when I heard you were up here

waiting for me," he said, his tone indulgent, almost loving.

"But I wasn't!" She gave him an appalled look. "I don't even know you –"

"That can be remedied!"

She turned her back on him because she couldn't bear to go on looking at him, completely relaxed and enjoying himself, lolling on the bed, while her own feelings were in complete turmoil. He had no right to be so sure of himself!

"Just because I had tea with you, it doesn't mean that I want to have anything more to do with you!" She thought that sounded rather well and cast him a nervous glance over her shoulder to see how he was taking it. His disbelief made her look away again quickly. "If you'll tell me where Mark Adeney lives, I'll go now!"

"What do you want with Mark Adeney?"

She shivered. "I don't see that that has anything to do with you!"

"You'll tell me all the same!" The inflexible note in his voice reminded her that his view of women was not the one she had been brought up with. It was all of a piece with the way he had kissed her – and who knew what else he might not do to her? It was unfair that he should be so attractive at the same time!

"He's my employer's brother-in-law," she said in a low voice.

"Did she send you to find him?"

Madeleine shook her head. "Nobody would give her his address."

He moved off the bed and in a couple of strides was standing beside her. With a hand on either shoulder, he turned her to face him, forcing her head up with a couple of fingers under her chin. There was no mockery in his expression now and she was very afraid of him.

"But they gave it to you?"

She swallowed convulsively, but there was no escaping his

38

grasp. "The hotel manager rang up the University –"

"Why?"

"When I got back to the hotel Mrs. Adeney had gone – taking all my belongings with her!" Tears of self-pity fell unbidden down her cheeks. She sniffed helplessly and tried half-heartedly to escape his hold on her chin. If she had expected sympathy, however, he had none for her. His fingers bit into her flesh as he forced her gaze back to meet his.

"Not much of a loss!" he drawled.

"It was to me!" she declared. "She brought me here – and she just went without a word! She took everything with her, all my clothes, even my passport! The manager said she had gone to Ankara, but she might just as well have gone to the moon!" Her sense of injury got the better of her and she began to cry in earnest. "I *hate* people who weep all the time!" she added violently.

His lips twitched. "Oh, quite," he agreed. "Almost as bad as men who kiss and tell!" He released her, allowing his eyes to slide over her while she searched in vain for a handkerchief and finally wiped away her tears on the back of her hand. "Have you finished?" he asked at last.

She attempted a smile and nodded. "I *never* cry!" she claimed, flying in the face of the evidence on her face. "I can't understand it! I must be tired – or something. I'm sorry."

He ignored that. "Wouldn't you have done better to find Mrs. Adeney rather than Mark Adeney?" he suggested.

"How could I? I couldn't stay at the hotel – that was made pretty clear! – and I haven't much money, and *she* has my passport!"

The mockery was back in his eyes, making her uncomfortably aware that his dressing-gown was not the ideal garment for her as it had been designed for a much larger person. "I didn't know this was your house!" she added on a note of desperation.

"I'm disappointed," he said dryly. "Though it's not surprising you were sent to this address. I am Mark Adeney."

"But you can't be!" In her consternation she lost her hold on the dressing gown and there was a flurry of activity while she retrieved the situation to her complete satisfaction. "The guide called you Maruk Bey!" She stared at him accusingly. "Where is Ursula, if you're Mark Adeney?"

"Good lord, I don't know, and I most certainly don't care!"

"But you must know! She can't leave me stranded in Istanbul like this! The least she could have done was to leave my passport and my fare home. You'll have to find her!"

To her annoyance he laughed. "I'm not going to find her! I've just spent the most uncomfortable week avoiding her –"

"By pretending to be someone else!" she butted in.

He shrugged his shoulders. "Ursula and I have nothing in common that I know of. It was my brother who married her, and a fine dance she led him. He bought out my share of the family business to please her, a fact for which I can never be sufficiently thankful, and when he died she inherited the lot. She's done very well by her own lights. Adeney Publications has become quite a money-spinner in the past few years. If she finds now that money isn't enough, but that she wants power and prestige as well, that's no concern of mine!"

Madeleine felt rather sorry for his sister-in-law. She looked about her for her handbag and a handkerchief, sniffing audibly.

"Your purse is over there," Mark Adeney pointed out. "It looks about as inadequate as the rest of your clothing!"

"That's why Ursula had my passport!" she explained.

"Very explicit. I'd as soon trust a rattlesnake with a newborn baby!"

"The London office sent me to look after her," Madeleine went on, feeling the need to reprove him but not sure how to accomplish it. "They're all very fond of her."

"Sycophants!"

She gaped at him. "Don't you like her at all?" she demanded.

"I wouldn't say that," he amended. "Let's say I can take her or leave her alone, but that I prefer to leave her alone. I don't like ambitious females."

Madeleine blushed. "I don't see that they're any worse than ambitious males," she said pugnaciously.

"That's because your ambitions lie in another direction, honey. It would never occur to Ursula that her role in life was to make some guy happy and follow his lead through life. I don't go a bundle on pushy women who drive their husbands into competing for more and more of the material things of this world until they fall into an early grave."

"I want lots of things!" Madeleine averred.

His smile mocked her. "If you were mine, you'd take what you were given and like it!" he retorted.

Madeleine pretended that she hadn't heard him. It seemed safer than going on with the argument. "Mrs. Adeney is a very good employer," she informed him. "I'll have you know –"

"Oh, wonderful!" he agreed dryly. "That's why you're in your present fix, I suppose? You forget that I know my sister-in-law pretty well. She came to Turkey to talk me into going back to the States to work for her, didn't she? Well, I'm sorry, but I'm not for sale."

"That's all very well," Madeleine said, "but it doesn't solve the problem of what I'm going to do!"

"Poor Melâhat!"

"And don't call me that!"

"You must be feeling better, you're getting quite bumptious." The glint in his pale grey eyes warned her to take care. "What am I to call you?"

"Madeleine," she stammered. "Madeleine Carvill."

"Well, Miss Carvill, it looks like you're stuck with the big, bad wolf for tonight at least." He smiled suddenly. "Madeleine! Who on earth called you that? I think Melâhat suits you better!"

"That's because you're conceited and – and –" Her voice trailed away and she gave him a guilty look.

"Yes?" he taunted her.

"And quite *horrid*!" she finished on a firmer note. "I think Adeney Publications are much better off without you!"

"Hear, hear!" he said with feeling. "Only that wasn't what you were going to say, was it? You're quite right," he added, "I did enjoy kissing you, and I may very well kiss you again!"

"That isn't what I was going to say at all!" She sat down heavily on the bed, her knees refusing to support her any longer. "What do you do?" she demanded. "What do you lecture about?"

"Architecture and the fine arts. Mostly architecture. That's why I came here to Istanbul. I'm writing a thesis on the Ottoman architect Sinan, if that means anything to you?"

She shook her head, then checked herself. "Yes, it does!" she said excitedly. "You told me about him in the Harem. Is he very famous?"

"Very," he agreed, amused. "He's the Christopher Wren of Istanbul, only fortunately the war didn't take the toll of his work that the bombing did in London."

She reminded herself that this was an American she was talking to. By comparison she had seen very little of the world and she was not sure that she had fully appreciated the little she had seen. "Do you know London well?" she asked uncertainly.

"I guess so."

She was silent. His knowledge of things Turkish had been so much more *explainable* when she had thought him to be Turkish himself. Now he had a whole new dimension added to him, that she had to allow for.

"Mrs. Adeney said you would be holidaying in the country," she remarked.

"I was until today." He glanced at his watch. "Yesterday. She wasn't far off the mark when she said what I was doing there either," he went on deliberately. "But she was wrong about one thing: I do not kiss and tell!"

Madeleine's cheeks burned painfully. "You mean you won't tell her about kissing me?"

He sat down beside her on the bed, pushing her loose hair back behind her ears. "Not worth the telling!" he teased her.

"You might not get the opportunity to tell her anything. She may have disappeared for ever!" She sighed. "What am I going to do?"

He pulled a lock of her hair very gently. "We could go back to where I first came in?"

She took immediate fright. "No, I couldn't! Please don't make me, M-Mar – Mr. Adeney."

"Mark will do," he drawled.

"M-Mark, then," she mumbled.

He ran a finger down her nose. "And don't look so worried, Melâhat! I don't seduce young women against their wishes. Especially when they're all eyes and nerves and in need of a good night's sleep!"

The relief was enormous. She didn't know why she should believe him, but she did, and she liked him more than ever for it. "I am rather tired," she said primly, and wondered why he laughed. She feigned a yawn and pulled back the bedclothes as a hint to him that she really did want to go back to bed and to sleep.

He took the sheet from her, giving her a push on to her feet. "This is my bed! If you don't want to share it with me, go and find your own. There's plenty of bedding in the closet in the bathroom and plenty of rooms upstairs. And, while you're about it, you can give me back my robe!"

Madeleine clung to the edges of the gown with resolution. "I haven't got anything else to wear! All your things are too big for me and I refuse to wear my own trousers in bed. The only *dress* I could find doesn't fit me either," she added, hoping to discomfit him.

She was completely unsuccessful. "It wouldn't suit you," was all he said.

She shrugged. "I can flip my hips as well as any belly-dancer I've seen in Istanbul!" she boasted.

His eyes filled with laughter. "Good! You'll have to show me some time. I don't think you'd relish the traditional payment for the accomplishment, though, so perhaps you'd better keep the robe until you get your own things back."

She put on an innocent expression. "Do you mean they get *paid*, as well as –?"

His hand came down hard on her posterior. "It's a man's world," he drawled. "In the old days he would put a gold coin on her forehead and her task was to go on dancing without letting the coin fall. Nowadays he puts a note in the top of her bra or, if he feels like it, in the top of her extremely brief panties. Now, are you going to bed?"

"Oh!" she gasped. "You're impossible!"

He raised his hand again. "Are you going?"

She fled, and the sound of his laughter followed her all the way up the stairs.

The top floor struck cold after the warmth of the lower part of the house. When the rest had been modernised, the upper storey had been left exactly as it had been when some Pasha from the past had owned the *yali*. The marble passages were freezing beneath her bare feet and none of the doors would open. She rattled the handle of the first door she came to, but it held firm. It was several moments before she realised that the latch was somewhere down by her feet and then, when she had got into the room, she found the bed was unmade.

She crept down the stairs again, her heart pounding. She had no ambition to run into Mark Adeney again that night. But his door was safely closed and there was no sound other than her own footsteps as she went into the bathroom and helped herself to as many blankets as she could carry. When she got up the stairs again, the door had blown shut, but she managed the latch with one foot and shoved at the door with her shoulder. She piled the blankets on to the bed and went over to the window to look out. She was higher over the water up here, but the strange noises of the waterway came clearly up to her window and the lights of Thrace shone brilliantly on the European side of Istanbul now that the rain had been cleared away by the light wind.

It didn't take long to make up the bed, which was old, with creaking, rusty springs that protested against her weight as she lay down. The room was very different from the one she had left downstairs. There were diamond patterns on the ceiling, ancient velvet curtains hung about with pom-poms, and wide-boarded wooden floors that creaked almost as much as the bed. It was, she reminded herself, the very first night she had ever spent outside Europe. This was Anatolia, Asia Minor, and a totally new continent to her. She smiled to herself in the darkness. The *yali*, especially this part of it, suited Maruk Bey far better than any setting she could have invented for him. It was odd that he should be an American and not the Turk she had thought him. Her heart jumped within her as she recalled the way he had of looking at her and she tried desperately to think of something else. In this she was aided by the throbbing engines of a ship making its way out of the Sea of Marmara, through the Bosphorus, up to the Russian ports of the Black Sea. It was a soothing noise and, listening to it, she slept.

There was no sign of the rain in the morning. The sun shone miraculously over the Bosphorus, burning away the last of the mists that clung to the little coves that indented the coast for as far as Madeleine could see. Oh, but it was a pretty place, this house of Maruk Bey's! She had had no idea when she had felt her way down the steps the night before how beautiful it was. It was made of wood, painted white in contrast to most of the other old houses that were blackened by wood preservatives

45

other than paint. Behind the house, the land sloped up steeply to the road. In front, the rooms hung over the water, hiding the boathouse at the bottom. The view was incomparable. Old Stamboul, with its skyline of domes and minarets, stood over to the left, crowding upwards towards Seraglio Point and the Topkapi Palace. Directly opposite was the new part of the city, a tangle of concrete and glass that clung to the steep hill without the romance of Stamboul, unless it was supplied by the waterside mosques and the Dolmabahçe Palace, the third and last of the Sultans' Palaces in Istanbul.

Madeleine dressed herself in her own clothes, glad that she would have the sunshine to warm her through the day. She wondered if Mark Adeney approved of women in trousers, not that she cared one way or the other, but she didn't want to be at more of a disadvantage with him than she was already. She had nothing else to wear, however, and though she could have wished that their wetting of the night before had not creased them, she thought she looked quite nice in them, especially with the bright, cherry red shirt that she was also wearing, a colour that she thought looked especially nice against the blackness of her hair.

She felt shy of seeing Mark again, remembering his parting thrust of the night before. She had not managed to dent his armour, while his effect on her had been devastating and complete. It simply wasn't fair! Her colour was considerably heightened as she strolled nonchalantly into the dining room, attracted by the smell of coffee and warm, freshly baked bread that was filling the house.

"Good morning," she said. Her voice broke and she coughed, feeling more of a fool than ever.

He rose to his feet, his head a little on one side as he looked at her. His slacks were as pale as her own and beautifully ironed, and she thought his shirt was real silk, buttoned only at the bottom to reveal the strongly tanned skin of his chest.

The sight of him made the whole nest of butterflies in her stomach leap into frenzied flight.

"I see you slept well!" he drawled.

"Yes, thank you, I did." She hesitated. "Did you?" she asked awkwardly.

"I could have slept better. Your presence had a disruptive effect on my dreams, if you want to know. If you're going to stay for long, we'll have to find some other night-clothes for you other than my robe, or I shan't last the course!"

She had the vague notion that he was complimenting her, more, was handing her a weapon ready to her hand, but she had no spirit to pick it up.

"I *can't* stay here!"

"Where else will you go?" he asked unanswerably.

Madeleine considered the point gloomily. "I could kill Mrs. Adeney," she sighed. "There must be somewhere that I can go!"

Mark looked at her with something very like sympathy in his eyes. "Ursula makes us all feel like that at one time or another. Don't fret, Madeleine, you'll be right in with her when she gets back. You managed to find me, after all!"

"I wish I hadn't!" He considered her gravely, while she blushed in dismay at her own words. "I mean," she went on, stammering over her amended speech, "I only meant that it isn't a very comfortable situation."

"It has its compensations!" he said dryly.

"I can't think of any!" She sighed. She had much preferred him as an unknown Turk, who had some excuse for looking at a woman as though she were merely an amenity put on this earth for his pleasure. As an American, he had had no right to make her feel as helpless as a twig going over a waterfall in full flood. As an American, he should have respected her itch for equality in these matters, whereas she didn't feel equal at all! She didn't begin to know how to handle him!

"It's a splendid adventure for you!" he teased her. He sounded kind, almost as though he understood her quandary. "You may even enjoy it, if you'd allow yourself to relax a little. It won't be for very long. I rang up the American Embassy in Ankara, and Ursula is there right enough. She went there to see a friend, in such a state of excitement that she forgot everything else!"

"Including me!" Madeleine said.

"I think you may get an apology for that. Either she'll be back in a day or so, or she'll send your clothes and passport and enough money to get you back to England. I fancy, though, she'll come herself. Now that she knows where I am, it will be too good chance to miss."

Madeleine gave him a hunted look. "I don't want an apology," she snapped. "And I think you're unkind not to help her when she asks you to. She may be round the bend, but she is your brother's widow! Wouldn't he want you to help her?"

"I don't think he'd care either way," Mark answered.

"But she was his wife!"

"That didn't stop him from taking this assignment to Viet-Nam. If he dug deep enough, there was a chance that the Government would sit up and take notice of Adeney Publications. His death has made no difference to that! Ursula can't wait to move in on Washington and she thinks I can get her there."

Madeleine knew nothing about American politics, but she thought that she understood what he was talking about. Only what had *he* to do with the seats of power?

"Can you?" she asked abruptly.

"Oh, I'm no politician!" he admitted. "But I'm pretty well known in my own field and I have friends where it counts. Ursula is no fool about that sort of thing, only this time she's misjudged her man. I don't want anything she can offer me. There was a time when I might have felt differently, but –" His lips twisted into an amused smile – "that was before yesterday."

"What was special about yesterday?" she demanded.

"I got something in my eye," he said with a chuckle. He laughed all the harder when he saw the blank expression on her face. "Never mind, Madeleine, I'll explain it to you some day."

"Yes, but what about her friend in Ankara?" Madeleine persisted.

"That is a new and interesting development," he agreed. "With any luck he'll give Ursula something else to think about and she'll leave us alone! I have enough on my plate just now, without Ursula nagging me to death!"

"But that won't help me!" Madeleine sighed. "What am I supposed to do?"

"Have you ever done any research?" he asked her.

She shook her head. "I'm a shorthand-typist." She averted her face from his interested eyes. "My shorthand isn't much good," she added with painful honesty, "but I type quite fast and accurately."

"Splendid! A stenographer is just what I need. If I work you hard enough you won't have time to get into mischief and I might get something done. Are you willing to work for me?"

She nodded, scarcely daring to breathe in case he changed his mind. "I'd love to! What do I have to do?"

"Well, some time you can get my notes into some kind of order. But first of all you'd better read up something on the subject and get to know the various terms I use. I think you'll find Sinan an interesting guy. I rather envy you discovering him for the first time."

She gave him a shy look, hoping that her pleasure wasn't as obvious as she felt it must be. "I haven't got my typewriter with me," she said.

"There's one in my room upstairs. I think we'll begin with one of the side benefits of research, though. Have you seen St. Sophia yet?"

Her eyes widened. "I haven't seen *anything*!"

"Nothing?" His smile mocked her eagerness. "Then we may

as well begin a few centuries before Sinan came on the scene. There's a church I want you to see first of all. It'll give you an idea of what Ayasophia looked like in the heyday of her glory, and I'll explain the alterations Sinan made to turn Justinian's Cathedral into a mosque. It was a watershed in Moslem architecture and had a tremendous effect on all Ottoman buildings everywhere."

Madeleine was highly excited at the prospect, but then she thought that it would be no part of his researches to go to such a well-known place. He had probably been there hundreds of times!

"You don't have to take me anywhere," she made herself say. "I shan't mind doing your notes without actually seeing the places myself. I can go later by myself. I prefer to earn my keep –"

He picked up her hand in his and his touch was very gentle. "Put your prickles away, Melâhat. They don't cut any ice with me! I want to take you and so we're going. Okay?"

She swallowed. "Okay," she agreed.

CHAPTER IV

"Do you think you may be cold?" Mark asked her as she came dreamily down the stairs, dangling her handbag between her fingers.

Madeleine shook her head. She was sure that she would never be cold again. It was a lovely day and she was about to do what she most wanted to do, she was going sightseeing in Istanbul! Mark could call it work if he wanted to, but to her it was a dream come true. That his presence was bound to make the whole thing much more enjoyable than otherwise, she preferred not to dwell upon. She had wanted to see the sights of Istanbul long before she had met him in the Topkapi Palace!

"How did you come by this house, Mark? It's perfect! Who lived here in the past? Were they very important?"

He shrugged his shoulders. "Some retired pasha, I expect. This is the *salemlik* down here. When the men had their friends in to visit with them, the women would be banished upstairs to the *haremlik* where you're sleeping. Are you warm enough up there?"

"Oh yes!" she assured him. "I took a pile of blankets up with me. I rather like it, that it hasn't been modernised like the rest of the house. I like the lattice shutters that cover the windows. It gives one a sense of privacy and yet you can see everything that's going on!"

He smiled. "Very romantic! I prefer central heating myself. I'll get Mihrimar to light the *tandir*. It usually gives out heat and smoke in about equal parts, but it will be preferable to you freezing to death!"

"Is that that kind of lotus blossom-shaped brazier? I think

51

I'd rather not! You forget that I'm British and used to the rigours of a real winter. Why, this could be an English summer's day!"

He accepted her verdict on the *tandir*. "If the English winter can turn out a complexion like yours, I guess it has its points," he added, watching the inevitable blush that crept up her cheeks with all his usual mockery. "Are you ready now?"

The last thing she wanted was to keep him waiting. There was always the chance that he might decide not to take her with him after all and she was very much on her best behaviour as she preceded him out of the front door and ran lightly up the steps to the road. It looked different in daylight. The shadows of the night had disappeared and although the Asian side of the city was poorer and shabbier than the European side, it also had a greater share of the old wooden buildings that had once been such a feature of Istanbul. Overlooking the waters of the Bosphorus were other large houses, many of them in a state of sad disrepair, which had once housed some of the grandest in the land. Huddled behind them, on the other side of the road, were the box-like dwellings of the poorer citizens, many of them wooden too, patched with orange-boxes and the like, but all of them scrupulously clean despite their multitudinous inhabitants.

"Mihrimar lives over there," Mark told her, pointing out one of the smaller houses that was approached up a steep, dangerous pathway. "These houses are all under preservation orders now because there are so few of them left. The ironic thing is that one is no longer allowed to build in wood in Istanbul. They had so many fires in the past, and these old wooden houses go up like tinder wood!"

Madeleine kept an eye on the broken pavement in front of her. "Why did you paint your house?" she asked him.

"The *yali*? I only rent it on a yearly basis. I got the landlord's permission to cover it with an anti-fire substance. D'you like it?"

She nodded enthusiastically. "I thought one of those ships was going to come right in my window last night!" she confided.

"They tell some pretty harrowing stories of ships that did just that to other people's windows. The Black Sea has very little salt in it, which means that a current pulls back into the Sea of Marmara, going against the lower current that flows the other way. It makes the fishing good, but it also means a great deal of mist and some pretty tricky navigation hazards. Don't ever go on the Bosphorus by yourself, Melâhat, or I'll have your guts for garters!"

She didn't mind his threat because it sounded as though he thought she was going to be in Istanbul for some time and that gave her a pleasant, warm feeling that she would examine at her leisure, when he wasn't there to distract her.

"Are there any important buildings in Üsküdar?" she enquired as they reached the ferry wharf.

"A few. There's the Mosque, or Cami of Atik Valide, by Sinan, and a couple of *türbes* by him as well."

"What's a *türbe*?" she asked.

"A mausoleum. I think he was the architect for the Semsi Ahmet Pasa Mosque too. He certainly designed the *türbe* there."

Madeleine's attention wandered to the ferry that was going to take them across the narrow strip of water to Europe. "Please may I buy the tickets?" she demanded, joining the queue with relish. She came back a minute or two later, triumphantly brandishing the tickets. "It's easier going this way!" she told him. "I didn't think I was ever going to get here last night!"

She made no effort to interfere, however, when they got to the other side and he shot her into a passing car that slowed to a snail's pace beside them, the driver shouting out some quite incomprehensible direction. There were already two passengers in the taxi, sitting in complete silence, and there was only barely room for them both in the back seat.

"How did you know he would take us?" Madeleine whispered, indicating the driver.

"It's a *dolmus* taxi. Haven't you been in one before?"

"No," she said. She eased herself away from him on the slippery, plastic-covered seat, and concentrated on the streets they were rushing through, nipping here and there to the constant accompaniment of the horn. Every now and again the car would slow down and one of the passengers would hand over a few coins to the driver and alight, but his place was always taken again almost immediately. It would seem that the Istanbulus either had very acute hearing or second sight, for they seemed to know by instinct where the taxi was headed for.

The walls of old Byzantium came into sight, crumbling with age, but still magnificent in their extent and formation. Here, New Rome had set its limits, outgrown them, and had rebuilt the walls further out. Thus it was that St. Saviour in Chora, called without the walls, had eventually been included, if only just, within the containing wall of the city. One of the most famous churches in the world, it wasn't known as St. Saviour any more to any but the Byzantine purists. The Turks called it Kariye Camii and had turned it into a mosque, covering up the fabulous mosaics and frescoes that covered the walls of the monastic church. Now, it was a museum, magnificently restored and cleaned by the Byzantine Institute of America, a fabulous treasure refurbished and open to all who appreciate lovely things.

"But this was never built by Sinan!" Madeleine protested as they entered.

"Certainly not! Moslems don't allow representations of human or animal forms in their places of worship. They say that the otherness of God is only confused by such images, so, when they conquered Constantinople, they covered them all up to make them fit places for them to worship Allah. But I wanted you to see them first, before seeing St. Sophia, to give you a better idea of what that church must have been like when Justinian had newly built it."

"But if Sinan —"

He cut her off with a smile. "A building doesn't exist in a vacuum," he told her. "Sinan restored St. Sophia, rather well in my opinion, and it in turn had the most tremendous effect on all his work. This church was built on the site of the ancient original church, about which very little is known. Maria Doukaina, mother-in-law of the Emperor Alexius I Comnenus, set it in hand between the years of 1077 and 1081."

"A woman?" Madeleine exclaimed.

"Why not?" he observed with mock condescension. "Women often inspire great works of art. Perhaps you will one day yourself; Melâhat!" he added deliberately, blatantly enjoying her mixed delight and embarrassment. But, after that, he allowed her to admire the mosaics in peace, only explaining the symbolism behind the gold-glinting ceilings and arches. "In Chora means in the country, which the church was, but it represents Christ as the 'country' of the Living and His Mother as the 'dwelling place' of the Uncontainable. You can work it out for yourself as you go round."

Madeleine did her best to follow his instructions. She felt quite dizzy with staring up at the roof above her, and even more reluctant to leave the sensitive portraits of Christ, the Virgin Mary, and the panels that showed their ancestors and the various incidents of their lives. She felt quite drunk with beauty when Mark finally insisted that they should leave. He had opened a whole new world to her and she would have liked to have thanked him, but she was too shy to do more than hurry after him, anxious not to be a burden on his own pleasure in the place.

"Mark, what brought you to Istanbul?" she asked him, as he pushed her into another *dolmus* taxi, keeping his hand lightly on her arm to protect her as they were flung from side to side as the taxi raced along the one way streets back into the old centre of the city.

"It was the furthest place I could get to from New York," he answered. "And I was interested in the place. You might say I was a bit fed up with the New World and thought I'd try the Old World for a bit. I came here at the invitation of the Boga-ziçi Üniversitesi – the University of the Bosphorus – to lecture for a year while I took my sabbatical year off from my job at home. But I guess I'll stay on for a while. If I can."

Madeleine bit her lip. "If Ursula allows you to," she burst out. "That's why you were avoiding her, wasn't it? And now you'll have to meet her, to get rid of me!"

Mark's glance was inscrutable. "Ursula is my problem," he told her. "I can look after myself, Miss Carvill. I wasn't look-ing to run into my sister-in-law, but it's a long time since any woman had the running of my life. I think I can cope with Ursula Adeney, or *anyone else!*"

Madeleine considered this. "You dropped me fast enough when you heard that I worked for her," she said finally. She hoped that none of the hurt she had felt at the time sounded in her voice.

He looked at her, his eyes amused. "Much good that did me! I didn't think you were worth having a row with over Ursula, but your persistence in following me home has made that inevitable. It could be that I underrated you."

"I didn't follow you!" she exclaimed.

"Nor did you wait to be asked!"

"I didn't know it was you! If I had I'd have – I'd have gone to prison first!" she claimed. "How was I to know that you were Mark Adeney?"

His smile deepened as he looked away from her. "Some-times I wish I weren't," he remarked.

She thought that Ursula must be a brave woman to tangle with him, certainly she would never have the courage to try and make him do anything he didn't want. She couldn't imagine him paying any attention to any woman who tried to divert him from his chosen course. That wasn't his way.

56

"I'm sorry," she said aloud.

"I know you are!" he observed. "Maruk Bey was a much more romantic person!"

She drew herself up with dignity. "I'm not a schoolgirl," she said. She paused to see if he had heard what she had said, and then rushed on, "Besides, you might just as well be a Turk! You have a very oriental view of women!"

"And what is that?" he encouraged her.

She wished that she hadn't said anything. "I daresay Ursula knows a great deal more about publishing than you do!" she told him.

He shook his head. "She doesn't. Though you're right about one thing. If she did, I still wouldn't take orders from her. Satisfied?"

"Why should I be? I don't care what you do!"

"Ursula uses power in ways I don't approve of. Bob couldn't handle her when he was alive, and I haven't the inclination to try—"

"Of course not!" she said. "You wouldn't approve of any woman who wasn't prepared to lay herself *flat* at your feet!"

He raised an eyebrow. "What's your objection?" he mocked her.

"There are women —" she began.

"There are indeed," he agreed promptly. "I number some of them among my friends. I don't happen to want to be friends with most women. I prefer a quite different relationship!"

"With you as master —"

"I'm a man," he said smoothly. "I'm fairly easily pleased, I believe, but I think it's the man's part to take the initiative between the sexes. You were born to be the quarry, Melâhat, not the hunter. It's one of the nicest things about you!"

She knew that he was teasing her and his words aroused a breathless excitement within her that told her it was only too true. "I haven't your experience, of course," she said with daring, "so I shouldn't like to generalise!"

"Quite right," he approved. "It's much better not to force an argument you don't want to win. There are other ways of finding out what you want to know. But drop it for now, there's a good girl, or you may find yourself right outside your depth. Okay?"

She knew a moment of painful indecision, tinged with fear. She thought she had been out of her depth ever since she had met him. In some ways she even enjoyed the sensation.

"I'm not trying to argue with you," she managed.

"I'm glad to hear it," he said dryly.

St. Sophia – Holy Wisdom – was something she felt she could do with. She waited for Mark to pay the taxi-driver, impatient to enter the building, expecting she knew not what, but sure that it was going to be one of the great experiences of her life because he had said the building was magnificent. When they did go inside, however, dodging the vendors selling postcards and other fripperies all round the gate, she was hard put to it to hide her dismay and disappointment. It wasn't what she had expected at all. It was dark and grey – and she didn't like it!

Mark's amusement at her reaction was very hard to bear. "If you want to see it as Justinian saw it, you have to cover the walls with mosaics in your mind's eye. Then you'll understand his triumphant exclamation that he had built better than Solomon!"

She tried to do as he suggested, but she was far too awed by the amazing proportions of the buildings. She felt dwarfed by it rather than uplifted, the weight of the pillars bearing down on her.

"I wish Sinan had built the whole thing," she declared.

"You'll get used to it!" Mark encouraged her. "Try and see it as a church first, then as a mosque, and not as a museum at all."

This she found much easier. In fact she liked the building

58

much more piecemeal that she did as a whole. She could admire the enormous green banners that proclaimed the names of Allah, Mohammed, and the first four Caliphs of the Moslem religion, if she separated them from the blue haze of tiles that decorated the walls and dome. She had to keep telling herself that the building dated from the year 532, and yet was the fourth greatest church in the world, with only St. Peter's of Rome, the Cathedral of Seville, and the Cathedral of Milan being larger. It was hard to believe that it had been conceived and shaped five hundred years before the Normans had come to England.

She wandered round the building, trying to concentrate on Mark's bits and pieces of information, as to which of the pillars had come first from Heliopolis, Ephesus, Baalbek, and even Delphi, from all over the Eastern Empire in fact. "O Solomon, I have surpassed thee!" indeed!

In front of the *mimber*, the marble pulpit used at prayers on Friday, stands the *Omphalos*, the "navel of the world", a mosaic of rare stones which was used for the coronation ceremony of the Byzantine Emperors. The sun in the centre, surrounded by six lesser planets, where stood the most important in the land. No women were allowed there, of course; they had a balcony to themselves at the back of the building, much as women still sit in enclosures at the back of even the most modern mosques.

"They didn't have much of a view," Madeleine remarked.

"Public life was not their natural sphere," Mark answered. His smile mocked her. "At times they ruled the whole Empire, but they were better off confined in their homes, making their husbands' lives more bearable. They were usually better loved in those circumstances."

"And to be loved must naturally be everything to a woman!" she retorted.

"To some women," he said.

"It isn't to Ursula!" she protested.

"Isn't it? It has always seemed to me that Ursula's search for power and money has been a rather poor substitute for the love she has never found."

Madeleine's eyes widened. "Didn't your brother love her?"

"In his way. Bob was no match for her and she despised him for it. Women often do, you know."

"I don't! I believe in complete equality!" she said, and wondered why he laughed. "You think you know *everything*!" she burst out.

He grinned. "Ah, but as you pointed out, I have so much experience!" He put his hand on her arm in a companionable way. "Come and see my pet demons. They're safely imprisoned in marble so that they can't do any harm. Perhaps they are female demons, though I have to admit they have a rather masculine look to them!" He showed her the faces in the grain of the marble and told her they were there because they had tried to interfere with the building by terrifying the workmen and had been turned into marble by God at the behest of the distraught architects.

He left her then to wander about as she pleased as there were one or two things he wished to see again himself. She found two great water urns, made of alabaster, far too large to carry, and they appealed to her for she liked their shape and the little taps that had been built into them. But it was the famous "Perspiring Column" that held her imagination most of all. She knew that it was only because it was porous and therefore sucked up water from an underlying cistern, but she couldn't resist sticking her finger through the hole in the bronze plate and feeling it for herself.

"Hadn't you better find a husband first?" she heard Mark's voice ask behind her.

She turned quickly, putting her hands behind her back. "Why?" she demanded.

"In Ottoman times, the women used to come here to pray to conceive quickly," he said. "Some of them still do, though they're more reluctant to admit it!"

"Oh, really?" she said, afraid that she was blushing. But she was glad when he turned away, making for the door, for she was suddenly, vividly aware of what a son of his would be like, strong and straight, and with the same light grey eyes that could make her feel so aware of herself as a woman. And for the first time in her life she knew the sharp knife of jealousy as she thought of the unknown woman who would be the mother of that son.

"It's Mihrimar's night off. I'll take you out to dinner," Mark had said that evening. Madeleine had gone into an immediate tail-spin because she had nothing suitable to wear and she couldn't, and wouldn't, believe that her only pair of trousers and cherry-red shirt would do anything but make her conspicuous in any restaurant after dark. "It isn't that sort of place," Mark had tried to reassure her, but it had been a discomfited figure who had accompanied him back to the old part of the city and into the restaurant of his choice.

Now, when she looked about her, she saw that he had been right after all. There weren't many women in the restaurant, as there aren't in any Turkish restaurant, but those that there were all informally dressed, some of them even in trouser suits.

"It's too early for the smart crowd," Mark smiled at her. "Don't fuss, Madeleine!"

"It's awkward having nothing to wear!" she sighed.

"It would be if it were true," he agreed, allowing his eyes to travel over her shirt with all his usual mockery. "You look as sweet as an apple to me!"

The slightly intoxicated feeling that had enveloped her ever since she had met him made her feel positively light-headed. She hardly noticed the gypsy family who had come into the restaurant to entertain the patrons until a sudden blare of music brought her back to earth, and she was surprised to see a very well-padded old lady knocking out the beat on a tambourine with all the enthusiasm of a teeny-bopper. Next to her sat her son, nominally the leader of the group, his trumpet in his hand while he chided his wife for her inattention on his other side. The two dancers were evidently his daughters. They came into the restaurant proudly, their minimal costume revealing near perfect bodies as their long skirts whipped round their ankles.

It was plain to Madeleine from the moment that she first saw her that the prettier of the two girls was well known to Mark. She came immediately to their table, leaning over his chair, and talking lightly to him in Turkish, her eyes wide with pleasure that he should be there. Nor did he seem to mind her flirtatious ways. On the contrary, he seemed only too happy to respond to her compliments, kissing her cheek and laughing at everything she said.

The dancing was agreeable – in parts at least. Naturally the belly-dancer found a ready-made partner in Mark. She pulled him on to the floor, cavorting before him in ever-decreasing circles in naked – yes, naked was just about the right word for it, Madeleine reflected – invitation. She didn't even mind when he put his hands on her bare back and pulled her close to him. Another kiss and a laughing comment, and she was gone to find another partner. But she was back almost immediately, pulling Madeleine to her feet beside her and pushing her into the dance, showing her the famed back-bending motion which, together with the rotating of the hips, makes up the belly-dance. And Madeleine could do it, just as she had claimed she could. She had not the slightest difficulty in going through the movements and was rewarded by the pleased gasp from the dancer as she went to find herself a new victim, and by a look in Mark's light grey eyes that sent her racing for the safety of her chair and her neglected meal.

"Very nice!" Mark complimented her briefly. He stood over her, making her blood race, holding out a note to her. She shook her head wildly, her face scarlet. But he was not to be gainsaid. With an easy movement of his hand he had found the front of her shirt and had firmly stuffed the bank-note into the top of her bra, his fingers just touching the soft flesh of her breasts. "I told you what the payment would be!" he said.

She had no objection this time when the dancer reclaimed him. She barely noticed that he was gone. Even when they cleared the tables and the dancers jumped up on to them, threading their way along them, jumping from one to the other, to claim payment from their male customers, even then she could barely bring herself to raise her eyes higher than the plate in front of her. Nor did she have the remotest idea of what she ate. Indeed, it was only when they came out of the restaurant into the cool night air that she summoned up sufficient courage to take the note out of its hiding place and put it in her pocket. At least it was dark outside and he couldn't see her embarrassment, even though it was cold and she had no coat to prevent the chill from striking directly on her bare arms.

"If you'd like to walk along by the waterside, we could go across in one of the small ferries by the Dolmabahçe Palace," he suggested.

She walked silently along beside him, unable to think of a single thing to say. She liked to watch the lights dancing on the water and to see the enormous shapes of the visiting ships that were tied up along the wharf. But it was cold too, and her teeth were chattering as they arrived at the jetty by the palace, having walked what seemed to her like miles in the surrounding darkness.

He handed her into the small motor launch that was quite different from the larger ferries that left from beside the Galata Bridge.

"Why, you're shivering!" He opened his coat and pulled it around them both, allowing the warmth of his own body to seep into hers. "I'd forgotten that you have nothing on!" he added in the special tones of mockery that he seemed to reserve for her. "Why didn't you say something?"

"I couldn't," she said abruptly.

His teeth shone white in the darkness. "Poor Melâhat! You do take life seriously, don't you?"

"I try to," she said. She put her hand in her pocket and drew out the note he had given her, startled to see that it was a hundred-lira bill, which she thought was worth well over two pounds sterling. "You didn't have to give me this. You'd better take it back."

His hand closed over hers. "Don't be silly, Madeleine. I wanted you to have it. You were quite right about your abilities as a dancer!"

"That's why I don't want it! You may be able to buy the favours of those dancers, but you can't buy mine!"

His arm tightened about her, moving her deeper into the warmth of his coat. "Are you sure?" he asked her. His voice was silky and spelt danger in its smooth inflections. "Put the money away!"

"I won't!" Her own voice broke alarmingly and she pulled away from him. "I won't!" she repeated.

His head blotted out the crescent shape of the moon and his lips came down to meet hers, barely touching her at first, but then silencing her protests with a contemptuous freedom that she had no means of combating. His hand came up behind the back of her head, holding her closely to him. "You see," he said, "your favours are not unattainable after all!"

If she had had any pride at all, she told herself afterwards, she would have done something to escape from him then, but the humiliating truth was that she did nothing of the kind. With a little sob, her arms had gone up round his neck and she had strained even closer to him, glad for him to kiss her as much and whenever he wanted to. She thought, when she could think at all, that it was nice that he didn't fumble as the only other man who had ever kissed her had fumbled, as unsure of himself as she had been. Mark knew exactly what he was doing. He refused to allow her any freedom of movement while he took an unhurried toll of her lips. Only when he had finished did he release her, a slight smile on his lips. She opened her eyes with a sense of shock, the moonlight dazzling her as it shone on her face.

"We're nearly there," he said.

"Are we?" she said weakly. She made an effort to pull herself together, ashamed of the residue of delight that lingered on her mouth.

The warmth of his coat deserted her as he stood up. He took the bank-note out of her hand and restored it down the front of her shirt. "If you look at me like that, I shall kiss you again!" he threatened. He jumped out of the boat and reached down to grasp both her hands, pulling her up beside him. He touched her cheek, and she winced away from him, suddenly finding her tongue and the pride she had feared he had demolished for ever.

"You had no right!" she trounced him warmly. "No right at all! It isn't my fault that I have to be with you. You're the brother-in-law of my employer and I'll thank you to remember it! You may not like it, but that's how it is. I'd go now if I could – and it isn't my fault that I can't!"

"No," he agreed. "It isn't your fault, Miss Madeleine Carvill. Let's hope for both our sakes that Ursula decides to remember you sooner rather than later. Don't look like that, my dear. I won't kiss you again while you're in my charge, though I must admit I prefer Melâhat to Madeleine!"

So did she! In the privacy of her room, Madeleine could have wept for all she had lost. She would have given anything to feel again his lips against hers. What could have come over her? She sat in dismay on the edge of her protesting bed and wondered at herself. Surely she couldn't want to join the procession of women who had briefly entertained him in the past. Surely she, with her strong Western ideas on the equality of women, couldn't possibly want that?

CHAPTER FIVE

MADELEINE knew it was raining even before she opened her eyes. She could hear it spattering against the shutters, in complete accord with her own mood, a mood which had been with her all night, costing her much both in sleep and in self-esteem. There was one good thing about it. It provided her with an excuse for pulling the bedclothes further up her back to keep the draughts out and to pretend to oversleep. In actual fact sleep was as elusive as it had been all night, but she shut her eyes all the same and waited for drowsiness to overtake her. Only, just as had repeatedly happened before, she had a vivid memory of Mark holding her close against him, and Mark's lips parting hers with a mastery that set her heart pounding as hard now as it had then.

She couldn't face him again. Supposing that he *knew* how she had felt? He had little excuse not to when she remembered how she had clung to him, even if she had lambasted him afterwards with a belated and pathetic dignity that wouldn't have deceived a child! It wasn't as if she had known him more than five minutes either. She had known other men for ages and she wouldn't have allowed them to kiss her. Only she hadn't allowed Mark to kiss her either. He just had, and she hadn't had any say in the matter. He hadn't asked her — she couldn't imagine him asking any woman — he had pleased himself and taken her acquiescence for granted, just as though he were indeed the arrogant Turkish male she had first imagined him!

But that wasn't the real cause of her indignation. That lay in her own response. Far from demonstrating her much

vaunted independence, she had been firmly put in the place
that he had allotted to her – and she had *liked it* that way!
There must be some fatal flaw in her character that she could
be reduced to being no better than a harem favourite with
nothing on her mind but the ambition to please some man.
Well, she wouldn't dwindle into anything so spineless! She
would not! But she thought she would be wise to avoid his
presence until she had succeeded in chastising her spirit into a
better frame of mind. *Then* she would show him that he had
a female on his hands to be reckoned with! A female, more-
over, who could take him or leave him alone with the same
arrogance he had shown towards her!

Sleep had never been further away. She pulled herself out
of bed in despair and went over to the window to stare out at
the grey Bosphorus. It was not an apt setting for her to cultivate
her resolution. She thought with a shudder of the women who
had been dropped into those very waters, tied up in weighted
sacks, for no other reason than that they had bored their lord
and master. She would have liked to think that they had intrigued against him too, but she doubted if the opportunity
had come the way of many of them. There had been a cruel
side to the soft living of the Ottoman Sultans, as could be seen
in some of the titles the individual sultans had acquired: who
wanted to go down in history as Selim the Sot, or Murat (or
was it Mustafa?) the Depraved?

The thought of the drowning women depressed her. The
waters below looked cold and unfriendly, ruffled as they were
by the blustery wind coming down from Russia. It was quite
different from the sunshine of the day before, as different as
her own wintry mood. She turned away from the window and
looked at herself in the glass, displeased by her shadowed eyes
and the pinched, vulnerable look round her mouth. She would
have to get dressed and go downstairs some time, she told herself. Putting it off was only giving herself the opportunity to
frighten herself still further.

Only Mihrimar was about when she went downstairs. She was obviously surprised to see Madeleine, but she made her some coffee without being asked, and found her an old coat of Mark's to wear round the house. By means of an elaborate pantomime she managed to tell Madeleine that Mark had gone out straight after his own breakfast, but that he was expected back to lunch. She then went upstairs, busy about her own work, leaving Madeleine to mooch round the sitting room trying to reject the idea that she was lonely and that she would have given anything to have gone out with Mark, no matter what the consequences.

He had thought about her before he had left the house, however. He had set up the typewriter at a handy table and had left a pile of his notes by its side in an untidy stack. Most of them she could read quite well, but many of the terms were strange to her and she soon went in search of a dictionary and one of his easier books on the art of architecture.

By the middle of the morning she had persuaded herself that she was much better off working on her own. She was interested in Mark's thesis and, without his distracting presence, she was able to concentrate on the extraordinary Ottoman architect who was the object of his researches. Sinan, the contemporary of Queen Elizabeth I, has at least one hundred and twenty major works to his credit in Istanbul alone. Twenty-four mosques, twenty-seven *medreses*, twenty *türbes*, eight *hamams* or Turkish baths, four *imarets*, and three hospitals, all accomplished by one man in a period of about fifty years or so. A phenomenal career for anyone, but especially for a man of his time when modern techniques of building were virtually unknown, even with the help of an *atelier* that must have included many skilled architects. Yet these are only his extant works in the city; others have long since been pulled down or totally reconstructed. Nor do these include his other buildings in various parts of what was once the Ottoman Empire, some of them as grand and as renowned as those he built at home.

Mihrimar came down the stairs giggling. Madeleine went out to the kitchen to see what was the matter, to find the maid busily ironing a pair of clean pyjamas for Mark. Another elaborate pantomime indicated that she had not expected to find Madeleine sleeping on her own in the old harem quarters. It was yet another indication of how Mark usually treated the women who stayed in his house! With her colour raised, Madeleine went back to her work and tried to concentrate once more on Mark's notes. He was worse than Don Juan and with as little heart for his victims! It was more than time that someone stood out against him, and she was just the person to do it. She would make sure that she was never alone with him again, even if it did mean that she saw nothing more of Istanbul, not even such wonders as Mark was willing to show her in the course of his trips round the old part of the city in search of Sinan's major works.

The strength of her resolution took a downward dive, however, when she heard him come in the door. She willed herself not to look up, or greet him as she longed to do. It was an effort to make her fingers go on tapping the keys of the typewriter as though nothing had happened, but, apart from the deep betraying blush that rose from her neck to brow, anyone might have concluded that she still supposed herself to be alone in the room.

The silence grew unbearable and she turned to find him studying her back with an interested air that didn't deceive her in the slightest.

"I was cold," she said weakly. "Mihrimar lent me your coat." She hugged it to her, unaware that the bright blue of the imitation fur lining set off her dark hair to perfection. "Do you mind?"

"Not at all," he said. "I've become resigned to sharing my wardrobe with you. I gather that my only clean pair of pyjamas are being hastily ironed for you to wear tonight. Mihrimar is convinced that it will be some consolation to you for being banished to the upper regions of the house on your own."

"I gather that it is – unusual!" Madeleine returned with spirit.

"Unheard of," he agreed dryly. "Did you expect it to be otherwise?"

She shivered, despite his coat. "No."

He leaned over the back of her chair, looking at her neatly typed pile of notes. "Don't make too much of it, my dear," he advised. "I'm not a monk –"

"I should think not!" she gasped.

"But neither am I quite the Lothario of your imagination. So you can put your hackles down and tell me what you've been doing with yourself all morning. You seem to have done a prodigious amount of work on my notes."

She eyed him suspiciously, wondering if he knew that she had been at a loss without him, lonely and restless despite all the resolutions she had made about him. "It's none of my business what you do!" she declared.

He laughed at that. He might as well have said that she would like it to be, because it was written so clearly on his face that that was what he thought. "None at all!" he said, with all his usual mockery. "And I don't like being taken to task by a chit of a girl for something which is none of her concern, so we'll let the subject drop, shall we?"

"Oh, I wasn't – I mean, I didn't think –" She was appalled by the conclusion he had drawn. "I expect they like it!" she assured him anxiously.

"Oh, Melâhat, you never stop to think, do you?" He smiled at her burning cheeks, running a gentle finger down her jaw-line. "I rather wish I hadn't promised Miss Carvill I wouldn't kiss you again for the moment. You make it so tempting to see if you wouldn't like it too!"

"I wouldn't! I don't like that sort of thing! I prefer to be asked!" She flounced across the room as far away from him as she could get. "And I may be only a girl, but I'm not a chit, and why shouldn't I take you to task if I feel like it? I have likes and dislikes and *feelings* too, you know!"

"Then you'd do better to keep them under some sort of control," he said lazily.

"You don't mind taking me to task!" she added. It was better, she discovered, to be angry than immobilised by the attraction he had for her. "You're always telling me what to do!"

"Oh, not the equality bit again!" He shook his head at her and his eyes no longer looked amused, but held a look that frightened her. "Listen to me, Madeleine, because I'm not going to say it again. There's no such thing as equality between us, and that has nothing to do with sex. It's because we're the people we are and you're not going to change that by throwing down the gauntlet whenever I come near you. You may make me forget that you're my sister-in-law's employee and, if you do, it will be you who will regret it. That battle would have everything to do with sex, and you would be destined to lose it as surely as night follows day, because you are a woman and I am a man. Meanwhile if I tell you what to do, you'll do it, and you'll put your feminine wiles away until Ursula chooses to remember your existence." He laughed shortly. "What happens after that is written in the stars, but I fancy you'll find yourself a better follower than a leader when we finally do come to terms!"

She was shaken by his vehemence. "I hate you!" she burst out.

"Oh, how you wish you did!" he observed calmly.

"I do! *I do!* I think you're unkind too!"

He held out a hand to her, picking up the notes she had typed for him in the other. "Did you work on these all morning?" he asked her. "If you go on as well as you've begun, I'll give you a credit when I publish my paper on Sinan. I hadn't realised what a difference a good stenographer can make to this kind of work!"

She went reluctantly over to stand beside him, pleased des-

71

pite herself at his praise. "Will Adeney Publications be publishing it?" she enquired, recognising that he was offering her some kind of olive branch.

He frowned. "I guess not. I'd prefer some other imprint."

"You don't give an inch, do you?" she complained.

"Not as far as Ursula is concerned." He clipped the pages together and returned them to the desk, smiling at her, his eyes crinkling at the corners in a way she had not previously noticed. "Are you hungry? Because I think Mihrimah is about to produce some lunch."

Madeleine sat opposite him at the table, her back as straight as a ramrod and her eyes carefully lowered to her plate. Her appetite had not yet recovered from the trouncing he had given her and she had no wish to bring herself to his attention again. When she felt him looking at her, she braced her shoulders to meet his gaze and smiled her most social smile.

"Why do the Turks call you Maruk Bey?" she asked him, pleased that her voice showed no signs of the trembling uncertainty within her.

He looked amused. "It's only quite recently that the Turks were made to have surnames," he explained. "It's still customary to call people by their first name. Maruk is merely their way of pronouncing Mark, with the 'r' sounded in the middle. Bey is a token of respect you give to a man you're not on intimate terms with. If you're speaking to a woman you add Hanim to her name. Melâhat Hanim, for example."

She gave him a shy look. "I thought you were Turkish at first," she said.

"That, my dear, was obvious!" he declared. "It was a touch of romance that I couldn't resist! It was a fine adventure for you to be picked up by a man from the east, though what you thought I'd do to you I can't imagine! Nothing that a good, red-blooded American couldn't do just as well! I was sorry, though, to disillusion you. It quite took the spice out of life

72

for you to find I am an American and as Westernised as yourself, didn't it?"

"If you are," she acknowledged, blushing a little. "You seem to me to have a very oriental idea of women!"

He laughed. "Never mind, Melâhat. If I have, you have the satisfaction of knowing that you are still *gözde*, a delight to my eye –"

"Me and how many others?" Madeleine hoped her tone sounded as light as she tried to make it.

His eyes swept over her, pausing for an instant on the top button of her cherry-red shirt and up again to the soft curve of her mouth. Apparently he was in no hurry to say anything. He was completely at his ease and he looked as if he liked looking at her, though she thought he had no right to make her so self-conscious of her body. Then, as suddenly, his mood changed, and he helped himself to some more of the excellent sword-fish Mihrimar had cooked with lemon and bay leaves.

"Would you like to take a boat trip up the Bosphorus this afternoon?" he asked her.

Madeleine's mind was in a whirl. She remembered she had decided not to go anywhere with him and she determined to refuse his invitation, kindly and with dignity.

"Yes. Yes, please," she said.

Madeleine had not been down to the boat-house before. It was like a great cavern beneath the *yali*, dark and rather scarifying.

"It has lots of atmosphere, hasn't it?" she said aloud, determinedly bright.

Mark turned his head and looked at her, a glint of amusement appearing on his rather serious face. "That coat would house at least three of you!" He watched her rising colour. "Come here and I'll turn up the sleeves for you."

She hesitated. For all she knew, it was the same coat that she had shared with him the evening before and that was an incident she didn't wish to be reminded about. On the other hand, it was difficult to manage when she couldn't see her hands at all, and the stiff material didn't give easily to her one-handed efforts at shortening the sleeves.

He was openly laughing at her when she went to him. "You look about six years old!" he said. "Especially when you look as though you expect to see a ghost coming out of the waters at any moment."

"There probably are ghosts down there," she insisted. "This house probably saw its share of the cruelty of the times. I was reading about it!" She shuddered, giving point to the horror story she was about to repeat. "Nobody was safe –"

"You should choose your reading matter with more care," he observed. "A nice, safe romance should be more in your line."

She looked down at his hands as he turned back the sleeves of the coat she was wearing, and thought how fine and strong they were. "It was a romance," she told him. "What could have been more romantic than Suleiman the Magnificent falling in love with Roxelana and making her his wife? Why was she called Roxelana? It wasn't her real name, was it?"

He finished his task, humping the coat up over her shoulders to give her greater freedom of movement. "The Turks knew her as Haseki Hürrem. The West called her Roxelana, or the Russian, because that was her supposed origin, but she was never known as that here. An Italian page in the Saray, called, I think, Bassano, said she was known by most people as the Cadi, or Witch, because they said she had bewitched poor Suleiman, he loved her so much."

"Despite all the other women in the Harem?"

"He put them all aside in her favour. Such is the power of a woman who is loved!"

She was suspicious of the amused note in his voice. She thought that he was telling her more than his words actually said.

"Did she use her power wisely?" she asked him.

74

"Not very. I think she must have had a jealous disposition, because she wasn't content that he loved her more than anyone, or anything, in his whole Empire. She had to have her own son follow him on to the throne and she persuaded Suleiman to murder his first-born son, telling him that the boy was plotting against him."

"I expect she wanted to be the Sultan Valide," Madeleine excused her. "She would have wielded more power as the Sultan's mother than as a Sultan's wife."

"Unfortunately for her, she died before her husband, and the Empire was left in the alcoholic care of Selim the Sot, the beginning of an endless decline into decadence."

Madeleine considered this. "I think it was Suleiman's fault," she said. "He shouldn't have given way to her!"

"That's an interesting theory from one who considers herself equal to any man."

"It was different in those days," she protested.

He raised his eyebrows. "Why?"

She shrugged her shoulders, anxious to end the discussion. Looking round the gloomy boat-house, her eye fell thankfully on the glistening bodywork of the motor launch. "How do we get it out?" she asked, stepping down into the cockpit with some difficulty because of the length of her coat.

But he had no intention of letting her off the hook. "Why?" he repeated.

"The ultimate responsibility was his. He was the Sultan. He had the actual power. All she had was her hold over him and if she used it to make him commit murder, that was his fault."

"Why?" he said a third time.

"Because a man should make his own decisions!" she retorted. "He shouldn't have let her get away with it!"

"Do I understand that you'd expect your husband to make his own decisions, even if it went contrary to your advice?"

"Of course," she said.

He stepped down into the boat beside her. "And what about the other way round?"

"It depends –" she began.

"On what? It's a simple enough question. Do you think a woman ought to set her opinion against her husband's judgement, or not?"

"I wouldn't put it quite like that," she said.

"I'll bet! Well, what's your answer?"

"I think if I loved him, I'd want to do whatever he wanted," she admitted.

He grinned at her. "Well, at least that's honest," he commented. "I agree with you. Suleiman should have kept Roxelana in better order. She probably would have liked it better that way, even if she had to put up with another woman queening it over her now and then. A little competition might have made her more appreciative of her good fortune."

Madeleine refused to answer. She helped him push the boat away from the landing stage and out through the lattice gates of the boat-house. Outside, she was glad to see it had stopped raining. A boisterous wind was blowing itself out across a wintry-looking sky, but it seemed as though the sun might come out and shed a little of its warmth across the grey, ruffled waters.

The engine leaped into life as the launch breasted the swell, sending a throbbing beat through the deck beneath their feet. It was a beautiful boat, with lovely lines, and very well kept. Madeleine wondered if it were Mark's own, or if he hired it along with the house.

"You agree with me?" he roared above the engines.

She peeped up at him through her eyelashes, giving him the victory. "Yes. But it doesn't become you to crow so loudly!"

He burst out laughing and she thought how very nice he was, when he wasn't getting at her. A ferry went by, giving the intermittent whoop-whoop on its hooter that had grown familiar to her as one of the sounds of the water. Madeleine waved to the seated passengers and was delighted when they

THE CRESCENT MOON

waved back at her.

"We'll go as far as Anadolu Kavagi and buy some fish," Mark said. "Further up is reserved for the military."

Madeleine was content to go anywhere. "Is it far?" she asked.

"It's about six miles from the end of the Bosphorus."

It sounded a long way. She gave a little sigh of content and sat back, leaning her shoulders against the top of the cockpit. It was pleasant to be out on the water and to feel the slight movement of the currents washing against the sides of the boat. On the Anatolian side of the Bosphorus, the *yalis* leaned over the lapping water in desolate splendour. Most of them, if they were inhabited at all, had been closed up for the winter, while their owners escaped the cold draughts of the Istanbul winter. Many of the houses were still made of wood, their roofs tiled dark red. Their huge, rambling interiors looked damp and neglected, though in August and September they became tinderdry and a single spark from a *tandir*, the open brazier that was all many families have in the way of heating, could send the whole place up in flames in an instant.

Interspersed with the older houses were newer ones made of stone. Mostly these were occupied all the year round, the owners commuting to the other side on the numerous ferries that stopped at the little jetties along the way, with their apple-green ticket office and waiting rooms.

"When the new bridge is opened next year, all these little villages will come to life," Mark said. "It's sad in a way. They may be administrated from Istanbul now, but they've retained their own character and way of life. They'll probably be eaten up in the end, like London has eaten up Chelsea and Blackheath."

"And New York?" she prompted him.

"New York is too busy tearing out its own guts to be a pleasant place to live these days."

"Then it isn't only because of Ursula that you don't want to

77

go back. Have you always lived there?"

He shook his head. "I gravitated there with the rest of the family. My people come from Connecticut. I still go back there sometimes, in the fall if I can wangle it, because there's nothing more beautiful in nature to my mind. You should see it!"

Madeleine felt at a loss, as she had before when he had told her about other places in the world. She thought again that she had been nowhere, and seen nothing, and that he would find that very boring if she were to spend long in his company.

"I don't suppose I shall ever see America," she said aloud.

He took his hand off the wheel, testing the wind with his finger. "It will all be there waiting for you. You've got a long life ahead of you in which to see the world."

She didn't believe him. "At least I'm seeing Istanbul!" she said.

"The Ford of the Cow," he smiled. "Did you know that that's what the Bosphorus means? Io, 'Inachean daughter, beloved of Zeus', was turned into a heifer to conceal her from Hera, Zeus's wife. But I guess the camouflage didn't work too well, for pursued by Hera's gadfly, Io plunged into the water that separates Europe from Asia. Hence the Ford of the Cow."

"It just goes to show that things don't change," Madeleine observed. "Even Zeus couldn't be content with one wife."

"He was a pretty unnatural fellow, with one of his daughters bursting out of his head, fully armed. Not the sort of person a nice girl would get involved with. You'd better stick to me!"

He turned the boat towards the bank and put in at one of the jetties. Huge plane trees grew almost to the water's edge, under which pink fishing-nets had been put out hopefully to dry. The fishing boats, mostly yellow in colour, had been drawn up against the shore, their owners taking advantage of the uncertain weather to sell the fish they had already caught. Beyond the village itself, the green of fields could be glimpsed, in which a few Genoese cattle browsed their way through the short afternoon.

"Are we really going to buy fish?" Madeleine asked, leaping neatly ashore and holding the painter he handed her with an abstracted air as she tried to contain her desire to explore the place they had come to.

"Mihrimar will be disappointed if we don't." He watched her tie the painter to a large ring in the jetty. "That knot won't do!"

"Then you tie it!" she commanded.

He did so, refusing to be hurried. "What fish do you like? Swordfish? Turbot? Or a *lüfer*?"

"I don't mind. Those all sound expensive, but I'll leave the shopping to you! I want to see what the village is like!"

Their walk through the village was pleasant. She liked the cobbled streets, the old wooden houses with their vine-covered patios, and the cats that crept out of the silent shadows intent on their own affairs. Mark took her into a tea-house and ordered a yoghourt for her and some tea for himself. The yoghourt was locally made, cold from the refrigerator, and with a delicious skin on the top.

"It's very Turkish to eat yoghourt by the Bosphorus, isn't it?" she said with satisfaction.

"Very," he agreed, his tone amused. "It's said to be very good for a lady's skin."

She avoided looking at him and made no complaint when he said it was time for them to be getting back to the boat. She stood beside him while he bought an enormous quantity of fish and stowed it away under the seat in the boat.

"Do you think you can cast off?" he called out to her.

She undid the knot he had tied so neatly and jumped hastily on board just as the engines started. "This is fun!" she exclaimed. "I'd love to have a boat! Does it cost a great deal to run?"

He nodded. "Quite a bit more than a car, but I find it more useful here. The public transport is both good and cheap – a very rare combination!"

79

They went back to the *yali* down the European coast. Mark pointed out the buildings of the University where he worked; Bebek, meaning baby, the most expensive suburb of Istanbul; the place where Barbarossa was honoured and buried; and the castle of Rumeli Hisar, the fortress built in three months by the Conqueror, or Fatih as he is called, to cut off any support from the Black Sea when he was beseiging the city in 1452.

"Rumeli is an old European name for Turkey," Mark explained. "Nowadays it's a favourite picnic spot in the summer. They perform plays there, and on Sunday afternoon they play the old martial music of the Janissaries. I'm told you can hear reflections of their tunes in Austrian music and even further west. Perhaps they were dinned into the heads of the Viennese when the Turkish army laid seige to that city!"

Madeleine would have liked to have heard it for herself. She was about to question him further when a gust of wind brought a new shower of rain sluicing down over the water, and she ran for cover under the wooden shelter that covered part of the cockpit.

"Just as well we're nearly home!" Mark grinned at her.

She nodded. She was sorry, though, that the afternoon was over. She found the *yali* on the opposite bank, its white paint gleaming against its dowdy neighbours. There was a light on in the boathouse and she looked enquiringly at Mark to find out if he knew it was there.

There was no doubt who was waiting for them, however, as the launch slid into her berth beneath the house. Ursula Adeney stood on the landing stage, her long legs a little apart and her hips jutting forward to emphasise her fashionable slimness. She made no effort to help them out of the boat. Indeed, she ignored Madeleine altogether, allowing her eyes to rest on Mark's impassive face.

"Well, I'm here!" she said.

CHAPTER VI

MADELEINE shed Mark's restricting coat, allowing it to fall in disorder at her feet. It was seldom that she disliked her fellow human beings, and she was surprised to discover that she was not at all pleased to see Ursula and that, somehow, it was all mixed up in the look on Mark's face when he had first caught sight of his sister-in-law. Of course Ursula was lovely to look at, more, she was beautiful, with her bright blue eyes and the colouring of a golden goddess. Any man would look twice at her! There was no need to dislike her because of that!

"You might have left my passport behind!" Madeleine shot over her shoulder. "What do you suppose the hotel thought?"

"Does it matter?" Ursula answered.

"*Matter?*" Madeleine's voice rose. "Matter? I should think it did matter! What was I supposed to do while you went waltzing off to Ankara?"

Ursula looked slowly round the sitting room and came back to rest on Madeleine's angry face. "You seem to have found yourself a very comfortable berth here," she drawled. "I shouldn't have thought Mark would have been so obliging, but perhaps he got something out of the arrangement too?"

Repelled, Madeleine glared at her. "You didn't think about me at all, did you?" she accused. "Did you realise that you had taken everything I possessed with you? Or didn't you care?"

Ursula smiled calmly. "I did forget about you for the moment," she admitted. "Something came up that put everything else out of my mind. I suppose I should apologise, but as you succeeded in finding Mark for me, I can't really say I'm sorry at all."

81

"Well, I'll have my passport now!"

"If you like." Ursula snapped open her handbag and produced the navy-blue passport, putting her own green one back in the pocket. "Though I do think you're making an unnecessary fuss, my dear. Nothing much could have happened to you, you know. They would have found me soon enough if you'd really been in trouble."

"Oh, that's too much!" Madeleine stormed at her. She took her passport with trembling fingers, tried to stuff it into her own handbag, found that the opening was still too small to accept the document, and flung it blindly on to the pile of notes she had typed for Mark. "You'll be telling me next that it was all for my own good!"

Ursula lit herself a cigarette. Madeleine noticed that she was completely calm. She snapped the lighter shut with an amused gesture, her blue eyes hidden for a moment behind a haze of smoke. "How do you get along with Mark?" she asked.

"All right," Madeleine said awkwardly.

"I thought he might have been making pretty speeches to you. He does, you know, to any pretty girl who comes his way. It doesn't mean anything."

The hot colour stained Madeleine's cheeks. "Your brother-in-law was very kind."

Ursula laughed. "Didn't he even kiss you? Oh well, I dare say he likes his women to be a shade more sophisticated, shall we say? How disappointing for you! I seem to remember that Mark kisses rather nicely. He has fewer inhibitions than poor Bob, who always treated me as though he were afraid I would break in his arms."

Madeleine allowed the remark to fall into a sticky silence. She gave a passing kick to Mark's coat and went and stood by the window, looking out at the rain-swept water below. The light was fading away from the sky over the Golden Horn, with none of its usual splendour. She could barely make out the domes and minarets of the famous skyline, and there was no colour anywhere. Everything was a uniform grey. The buildings, the land, the sky, even the water that separated the two parts of the city.

"Don't you approve of Mark having kissed me?" Ursula's voice needled her softly.

Madeleine shrugged. "It's none of my business what either of you do!" She cleared her throat angrily. "Except when it affects me. Why did you go to Ankara?"

"I heard a friend of mine was there," Ursula replied easily. "I wanted to see him very badly, so I took the first plane that was going. It it's any comfort to you, I had to pay a huge amount on your baggage. It was the first I knew that I had it with me."

"*Somebody* must have packed it," Madeleine pointed out.

"The chambermaid. She did mine as well, while I arranged about my ticket and checked out at the hotel. Are you still angry with me?"

Madeleine turned and looked at her. "Yes."

Ursula laughed, flicking her ash on to the floor beside her chair. "But why? I've explained how it happened!"

"You haven't begun to explain!" Madeleine retorted. "I'm sorry, Mrs. Adeney, but I don't feel that I can continue to work for you after this. I'd like to go back to London."

"That will be popular in the London office!" Ursula observed. "Have you thought that they may dispense with your services altogether if they think you've abandoned me as soon as the going got rough?"

"But I didn't! You abandoned me!"

Ursula drew on her cigarette, looking pleased with herself. "They *may* believe you –"

Madeleine went white. "Why shouldn't they?"

"Because I don't think I'd put it quite like that in my letter to them," Ursula said sweetly.

"That's the last straw!" Madeleine exclaimed, more angry than she had ever been. "I don't believe I've ever met anyone

83

more selfish, dishonest, and – and lacking in integrity!'"

But Ursula only laughed. The only sign of emotion that Madeleine could detect in her face was a slight hardening round the eyes, and even that disappeared when the door opened and Mark came strolling into the room, rubbing his hands on his handkerchief to dry them.

Ursula greeted him with a cosy smile. "Do you think I'm dishonest and lack integrity?" she asked him.

"Probably," he said dryly.

"How unkind! I expect you put the idea into Madeleine's head in the first place. She would never have said such a thing to me a couple of days ago."

"I hadn't cause to!" Madeleine snapped, her patience exhausted. "I don't care if I do lose my job –"

Mark stopped her with a look. "That's enough, Madeleine. Fire-eating won't help. I think you'd better leave it to me until you've cooled down and can think straight. Mihrimar could do with a hand in getting a room ready for Ursula." He turned in enquiry to his sister-in-law. "You are staying, I presume?"

"If you'll put up with me," Ursula said meekly.

Madeleine cast an outraged look at them both. "Don't you *care* –"

"Drop it, Madeleine!"

"But I thought that *you* at least –"

His hand came down on her shoulder and she found herself propelled towards the door and deposited on the other side, the door being firmly shut in her face. Tears of rage and humiliation drenched her face. She wiped them away with her hand, unconsciously listening to what they were saying on the other side of the closed door.

"If that's how you treat her, I'm not surprised she wants to back to London," Ursula's voice drawled with amusement. "Of course she's just a child! Still, I don't suppose she likes being treated as one!"

And then there was Mark's voice, cool, calm, and collected.

"This has nothing to do with Madeleine. This is between you and me."

Madeleine turned and ran up the stairs to her room. Great shattering sobs shook her as she flung herself on to her bed. How could he say it was nothing to do with her? Had it all meant nothing to him? Did he agree with Ursula that she was a child and could be safely treated as such? She felt again in memory his lips on hers and the emotions he had stirred within her with such masterful ease. Had he thought her response to be that of a child? But no, that she couldn't believe. She had felt him tremble against her even while he had held her. He had kissed her as a woman, not as a child, in spite of his complete domination of her.

She turned on her back, looking with unseeing eyes at the diamond pattern on the ceiling. If Ursula had known his kisses too, no wonder she had been disappointed in her husband's embraces. But Madeleine preferred not to think such thoughts. She got off the bed and nearly fell headlong over her suitcases. She fell on her knees beside them, forcing them open. At last she could change out of her trousers and cherry-red shirt and wear a skirt again, and in a skirt, she thought, she would look considerably less of a child, and she would feel less of one too! She would look every inch as suave and as cool as Ursula! There were considerably fewer inches of her, of course, and she would never look like a golden goddess no matter how she tried, but it was she that Mark had called Melâhat, not Ursula Adeney, and no one could ever take that away from her!

She chose a dress of heather-coloured Scottish tweed, tailored to fit every curve of her body, and wore her finest stockings and a mauve-tinged lipstick that accentuated her dark colouring and would have looked terrible on Ursula. She was admiring the total effect in the looking glass of the dressing-table when she heard Mihrimar coming up the stairs. Her footsteps sounded weary and Madeleine's conscience smote her. She had her own house to run as well as Mark's and her own coming had meant a great deal of extra work for her, without having Ursula staying in the house as well.

Madeleine went out on to the landing and took a bundle of bedding from the Turkish woman's arms. Mihrimar flung her head backwards in the Turkish gesture of denial and muttered something that Madeleine couldn't understand. She was obviously far from pleased to be doing housework at this hour of day and she had no hesitation in showing it. With a practised movement of her foot, she unlatched the door of the room next to Madeleine's and went inside, sniffing at the stale air of the long shut up room. She left it to Madeleine, however, to open the window and to push back the shutters, allowing the rain-laden wind to rush in, tearing at the ancient velvet curtains and sending the bedside light crashing to the floor. With a gasp of laughter, they both strove to fasten the shutters again, each of them exclaiming in their own language.

With some kind of order restored, Madeleine stripped the cover off the bed and bent to pick up the underblanket from where Mihrimar had thrown it on the floor. The mattress felt cold to her touch and when Mihrimar went and stood on the other side of the bed, the Turkish woman uttered an annoyed cluck of dismay and pointed towards the *tandir,* resigned to the fact that it would have to be lit to warm and air the room. She set off down the stairs immediately, leaving Madeleine to finish the bed, and came back a few minutes later, panting under the weight of the charcoal and kindling she had fetched from the kitchen.

Inevitably, smoke poured out into the room as Mihrimar strove to light the brazier with a quick, fanning motion that was supposed to make the kindling burst into flame. It wasn't very successful. Madeleine knelt beside her, making helpful suggestions in English that fell on deaf ears. Mihrimar went stolidly on with the business in hand, oblivious to the disastrous results of her efforts. But, at last, a small flame flickered and caught and the Turkish woman gave Madeleine a triumphant look and stood up, wiping her face with blackened fingers. She would have patted Madeleine on the shoulder too, but Madeleine stepped away hastily, pointing to her clean dress and to Mihrimar's smeared face in the mirror. The Turkish woman giggled and nodded.

"*Çok tesekkür ederim*," she murmured, glancing towards the bed. Her eyes twinkled with affection as she smiled. She gathered up the dusty remains of the bag in which she had brought up the charcoal and led the way down the stairs again, gesturing towards the still closed door of the sitting room. She pointed towards Madeleine's dress and giggled again. "Maruk Bey –!" She kissed the back of her hand and laughed once more. Madeleine blushed, and would have gone back upstairs to her room if it had not been for the maid's unyielding stance beside the door. She hesitated, feeling foolish, and Mihrimah opened the door herself and, with a last imperious nod of her head, nudged Madeleine into the room.

Mark stood up as she entered, his head a little on one side as he looked her up and down.

"I thought I'd change," she said abruptly.

"Very nice too!" he said.

Ursula patted the seat beside her on the sofa. "Is it my imagination or do you smell of smoke? How did you manage it? The central heating seems more than adequate to me."

"It doesn't go upstairs," Mark answered for Madeleine. "Is Ursula's room ready for her?"

Madeleine's eyes sparked with anger. It wasn't her business to get a room ready for Ursula, she thought. "The bed is made," she forced herself to say politely.

"By you?" Ursula drawled. "I thought you had a maid, Mark? That bundle of a woman who let me in."

"Mihrimar," he confirmed. "She has enough to do without making up beds at this time of day. She's getting old and has rheumatism in her knees."

"Is that why you let her wear a head-scarf in the house?"
Ursula asked, amused.

"No." His light-grey eyes were thoughtful and withdrawn.
"It makes her uncomfortable to uncover her hair in a man's
presence."

Ursula threw back her head and laughed delightedly. "You
don't mean it? The poor thing!"

Surprisingly, at least it was a surprise to herself, it was
Madeleine who rushed to Mihrimar's defence. "I don't see
anything funny in her keeping her crowning glory for her husband. Many of the women cover their mouths as well when a
man passes them in the street. They probably give much more
of themselves to their husbands and are much more faithful
than we are in the West. It isn't very long since they wore the
veil!" Her eyes met Mark's and she wished she had kept quiet.

"Her 'crowning glory'?" Ursula repeated. "My dear girl,
she's more likely completely grey and rather thin on top!"

"We all grow old," Madeleine snapped.

Ursula exchanged glances with Mark. "I suppose we do.
That's why I believe in gathering as many rosebuds on the way
as I can."

Madeleine saw a flash of amusement in Mark's eyes and an
uncomfortable conviction grew within her that she had walked
into something between them when she had come into the room.
Ursula opened her bag and drew out her lipstick, carefully re-
applying it to her lips. It was then that Madeleine knew, as
certainly as if she had seen them, that Mark had kissed her
and that he would like to kiss her again. She could see it in his
face and in the smug satisfaction with which Ursula put her
cosmetics away and snapped her bag shut.

"Men have their uses," Ursula went on, her blue eyes very
bright. "Women weren't made to compete in the hard world
of business, I'm convinced of that! I'm exhausted from the
struggle of trying to keep everything together!"

"You don't look it," Madeleine put in, unable to bring herself to look at either of them.

"But I am! Mark darling, I know I didn't behave very well to you in the past, but you're not going to make me plead with you, are you? I really need you in Adeney Publications, whatever I may have said when I was lost and unhappy, as I was when Bob was killed. I thought having something to do would give me an interest in life, but it hasn't worked out. Nobody pays any attention to a woman boss, not where it really matters. Take this expedition, for instance – I'm supposed to be doing a piece on Turkish carpets while I'm here, and they won't even take the time out to show me any. How d'you like that? We need you back with us, Mark. I've got to have you back!" The merest suggestion of a sob entered her voice and her eyes filled with tears as she looked helplessly up at Mark.

Madeleine gasped audibly. If she hadn't seen it with her own eyes, she wouldn't have believed that Ursula could look so soft and seductive! Or be as untruthful! How could she bring herself to use such weapons against Mark? All this tarra-diddle about Turkish carpets, when Madeleine knew for a fact that she hadn't lifted a finger to see anyone except her brother-in-law the whole time she had been in Istanbul!

"I shouldn't have thought Turkish carpets were much in your line," Mark said, standing up. There was a note of withdrawal in his words that Ursula was quick to pick up.

"Please, Mark! I'm at my wits' end –"

"All right," he agreed abruptly. "I'll write it for you. Madeleine can type it up in the morning, I suppose that's what she's here for, and you can send it in under your own name."

"Oh, *darling*, thank you! That's more than I dared to hope for! It's a splendid beginning –"

"It isn't the beginning of anything, Ursula," he cut her off. "You can call it the final payment on the past. Adeney Publications is all yours, my dear. I want no part of it. Is that understood?"

"You can't make me give up hope that you'll change your

89

mind," Ursula rapped out. "I won't ever do that! You haven't changed, Mark, no matter how much you think you have. I want you to know that when you finally get around to forgiving me, I'll be there, waiting for you. After all, the business does bear your name too!"

Mark's look was impassive. "There's no going back," he said. "I'll do this article for you, but that's it, and you'd better believe it!"

But Ursula only smiled. "I'll believe it when you can honestly tell me that you're no longer jealous of that big brother of yours, and I don't think that you can, not then, and not now!"

Mark was silent for a long moment, then he said: "Bob is dead, Ursula, and a lot of things died with him. Maybe Adeney Publications did, if you really can't run it on your own. I have my own life to live and, to tell you the truth, it's looking pretty good to me, and it has nothing whatever to do with you!"

Ursula pinched in her lips, moving her hands restlessly about her. "We'll see, Mark darling, we'll see!"

"Well, Madeleine, it looks as though we're going to find out how good your shorthand is."

Madeleine swallowed. "I told you it isn't much good! I'm not used to people dictating to me, but I'll do my best."

Mark leaned back in his chair and studied the toes of his shoes. "And you're prepared to have me dictate to you?" he drawled.

"It's my job!" Madeleine began, and saw him smile. "You'd better not let Ursula hear you saying such things!" she added. "She wouldn't think it at all funny."

"Where is Ursula?" he asked.

Madeleine's long lashes flickered down on to her cheeks, she was so anxious to hide her thoughts from him. "Upstairs. I don't think she slept very well last night. She felt stifled with the brazier going in her room, so I hauled it out on to the landing and then she was cold. She isn't used to the noise either. The ferries do start early. And the lights from the fishing boats disturbed her. I think she thought they were dope-smugglers."

"My word, you are in a superior mood! Don't any of those things bother you?"

She shook her head. "I like the rooms upstairs. They're so secure and safe somehow. You can see out, without anyone being able to see in. If it were my house, I'd never change them!"

"They may not be as safe as you think –"

She looked up at him at that, her eyes wide. "Nobody was drowned from this house, were they?" She couldn't quite put the picture of the drowning ladies of the harem out of her mind.

"Not so far as I know, but I expect harem politics went on here as intensely as they went on everywhere else. Maybe some of the women weren't too particular about the weapons they used to get what they wanted."

No, she thought, and it wasn't all in the past. Ursula wasn't at all particular for one! Did he know that? She thought he might, for he had never had the least difficulty in reading her motives, often before she had grasped them herself. So perhaps he was warning her? She looked at him reflectively, but he gave nothing away. He just went on looking at his feet. But then what had a woman's integrity ever had to do with a man's being attracted to her? Madeleine sighed and turned over the pages in her notebook.

"I'm ready," she said.

He looked up and his eyes met hers. "I'm no Suleiman, Madeleine. My brother was prepared to allow a woman to rule him for a while, but we never were much alike, whatever Ursula may tell you. When it comes down to it, I shall please myself and nobody else!"

She bit her lip. "I know you will. Does Ursula?"

He grinned. "Humph, not as defenceless as you look, are

you? Well, you can put your claws away for a bit while I knock out this article. Ursula is my business and nothing to do with you. As a good employee, your task is to keep us both sweet and to keep your own nose clean. Okay?"

She nodded, pencil poised over a clean page. "At least I've got my passport now, if the worst comes to the worst," she said.

"That's what you think!" he told her. "You left it on my notes and I put it away with mine. If you need it, you'll have to ask me for it, and you can blame your own carelessness for that!"

She refused to answer, bending over her work with a look of fierce concentration on her face. To her relief he began to dictate almost immediately, in a clear, concise manner that she found easy to follow. Her training made it difficult for her to take in the details of what he was saying at the same time as she took it down, but the snatches that came through to her intrigued her. How did Mark know all these things? He didn't refer to a single book or note during the whole session; the details poured out of him in an orderly torrent, starting at the beginning of the girl's training at the age of five in tying the knots, through her beginnings in making her own carpets when she was eight years old, to the time when she was eighteen and was already losing the facility in her hands to tie the thousands of knots that go to make up every hand-made carpet. He dealt with the making of the dyes, the working out of a design in the girl's mind, and even how to tell the different grades of carpets apart by turning the pile back and finding the knots, and how many there were to the square inch of carpet. He explained the use of the famous prayer carpets, which always included a pointer that was laid out in the direction of Mecca, and the gallery carpets that could be used by a whole family when they were saying their prayers.

"In Turkey," he ended, "everybody has fine carpets for their floors. The rich buy them and the poor make them."

"Does anybody oversee the girl when she's designing and making her first carpet?" Madeleine couldn't resist asking him.

He shook his head. "They are artists, and they are treated as such. There are certain recurring patterns, of course. The Tree of Life, for example. Or stylised tulips, fruits and flowers. Or some ancient folk design. It depends on the girl's own skill and whim, just as the depth and originality of the colours depends on her knowledge of dyes and their use. In their own field, these girls are Rembrandts, Van Goghs and Jackson Pollocks. Their extreme youth makes their achievements all the more remarkable, but unfortunately not more appreciated."

"You appreciate them!" Madeleine exclaimed.

"True, but then I have a horror of the machines taking over all the arts." He gave her a sly smile. "Though perhaps most of us wouldn't realise the difference," he added. "Not even the readers of Adeney Publications!"

"Some of them would," Madeleine insisted. "More of them will when they read your article!"

He shrugged, frowning. "They'll look at the pretty pictures, but shallow, glossy magazines are designed to give an illusion of civilisation, they have very little to do with the reality."

"Now who's being superior?" she demanded.

"*Touché*," he admitted. "Think you can get all that typed up today?"

"I think so," she said. "I'll be interested to read it properly. When one's taking something down in shorthand one becomes a bit of an automaton, at least I do. I hope you won't find too many mistakes in it, but I can always type it again tomorrow."

It took her most of the rest of the day to finish the article. Ursula tried to hurry her along by sitting in the sitting room with her and reading the pages as they came off the machine. Madeleine wished that she would go away, but as Mark seemed pleased by her interest, she felt she had to put up with her. It meant that she made more mistakes in her typing than she usually did, though, and her back ached with weariness when she finally clipped the pages together and handed them a copy each.

Ursula's excitement over the piece gave her a glow that made her lovelier than ever. "It's perfect, Mark! It's absolutely perfect! Oh, Mark darling, you must come back to New York with me and take over the group. I promise you there aren't any strings attached to the offer. I'll be as good as good can be and do exactly as you say! I've missed you, quite apart from Adeney Publications. I've missed you terribly! If you played your cards right, you could have me as well as the business. You wanted that once, and now it could all come true for you!"

Mark stood and looked at his sister-in-law. "You think so?"

"Darling, I know so!"

Madeleine tried to pretend that she was not listening to them. She put the cover over the typewriter and lifted it down from the table to put it away. When Mark took it from her, she thanked him briefly, but she couldn't help the sick dismay she felt in her stomach at the gleam of longing she thought she detected in his eyes.

"I seem to remember you singing another tune," he said to Ursula. He didn't sound bitter, or anything very much. He was as matter-of-fact as he had been when he had been dictating the article to Madeleine that morning.

"You're not going to hold it against me that I was bluffed because Bob was taller than you, are you?" Ursula pleaded. "I thought it meant he was taller inside too. I guess I was young and silly, Mark, but I thought it was what I wanted at the time!"

"It was. You wanted Bob, and you wanted Adeney Publications. You got them both. Bob forced me out. I sold out all my shares to him and with them all my interest in Adeney Publications. I mean that! You're whipping a dead horse, Ursula. I'm not going to run, certainly not at your say-so. You got what you wanted and you'll have to live with the results of that wish. It's none of my concern, and I don't intend that it ever shall be again!"

He smiled and bowed at them both, walked swiftly over to the door and was gone before either of them were aware. Seconds later, the front door slammed with a bang that echoed through the house.

"How dare he?" Ursula whispered through thinning lips. "How dare he? And what does he expect us to do all evening? Entertain ourselves?"

Madeleine looked at the closed door with a leaden heart. The prospect appealed to her as little as it did to her employer. "It looks as though we shall have to," she said. "I'll tell Mihrimar that there will be only two for dinner."

"Tell her what you like!" Ursula said bitterly. "If you can! She doesn't understand a word I say to her! What a hole this house is – and we've another freezing night ahead of us! There are times when I *hate* Mark Adeney, and I don't mind telling you that this is one of them!"

CHAPTER VII

URSULA retired to bed at ten o'clock on the dot. There was no
water on the upstairs landing, so she called down to Madeleine to bring her up a glass of cold water when she came up.

"I'm not spending another night like the last one for anyone!" she declared when Madeleine appeared in the doorway
of her room. "It's bad enough having to go to bed with the
birds, without freezing to death for our pains! I'm going to
take a couple of pills and make sure that I get some sleep!"
She sighed heavily. "Now what's the matter, honey? You've
been in the sulks all evening. You're not still holding it against
me that I had to go to Ankara, are you?"

"No." Madeleine handed her the glass of water and watched
her take the tablets from the palm of her hand.

"Want some?" Ursula offered. Madeleine shook her head.
"Oh lord, I suppose you don't approve, or something! How
apt that New England should have been called that! You're
exactly like my late mother-in-law, d'you know that? She'd
have died of lack of sleep, still claiming that of course she
wasn't tired! It took quite a while to get Bob to come round
to my way of thinking!"

"But you managed it?" Madeleine said quietly.

"Of course I managed it! Mark isn't doing himself any
favour by underrating me. I'm Bronx born and bred and in
this world, believe me, that's quite an advantage when dealing
with the Adeneys, and I've had quite a lot of experience in
doing just that." Her blue eyes rested lightly on Madeleine's
face. "Don't get involved, dear. You don't stand a chance in
my league." She pouted thoughtfully. "Nor does dear Mark.

He'll come back to New York in the end of the bait is made attractive enough."

Madeleine took the proffered empty glass with what she hoped was a suitably enigmatic expression. Without make-up, Ursula looked less vulnerable than she did by day, her mouth less full, and her eyes harder.

"Shut the door behind you, Mad honey. I can hear your bed creaking when you leave everything open."

"Good night," Madeleine wished her, her feathers ruffled by the contraction of her name. The latch of the door slipped under her foot and the door slammed shut in the draught. Madeleine tried to feel sorry that she should have made quite such an abrupt exit, but she wasn't sorry. It had been well in accord with her mood and had given her a satisfaction out of all proportion to its real importance. She only wished that a whole lot of other doors could be shut on Ursula Adeney as easily.

Her own room struck cold when she entered it. No brazier had been burning in it from early morning, and the raw, damp wind from the Bosphorus came roaring in through the open window. Istanbul in winter had its own attractions, but the cold wind from Russia was not one of them. Madeleine wondered if it ever brought snow to the city, but it seemed more likely that cold mists and leaden skies more usually came from that direction. In between were the dazzling, dancing days of sunshine and warm, black nights with only the crescent moon and stars like jewels to light the sky. Like it had been when Mark had kissed her on the ferry boat. She gave herself a mental shake. She had to remember that she wasn't the only person he had kissed. She made herself remember, coolly and rationally, Ursula's smudged lipstick of the evening before. Ursula, too, must know what it was like to feel her bones melt within her at the touch of Mark Adeney!

Sleep came only intermittently with such thoughts buzzing round in her mind. It seemed to Madeleine that the fluorescent hands of her watch moved hardly at all between the times that she looked at them. Midnight came and went, and one day slipped into the next, and still she could not settle into the deep, dreamless sleep that usually came to her without having to be wooed and made much of. One o'clock. Perhaps she would have done better to have read away this part of the night and saved her sleeping for later, but it was too late now to go downstairs again in search of a book. It was a matter, or so she told herself, of concentrating her mind on other things. If the worst came to the worst, she might even try counting sheep.

She barely heard the front door open. It must have been the rasp of the key as it entered the lock that had alerted her. A joyous feeling of delight fountained up within her. Mark had come home. She was out of bed before she had thought, her feet searching for her slippers at the same time as she struggled into the wispy nylon dressing-gown she had brought with her because it packed easily. She went flying down the stairs, her eyes bright, all thoughts of sleep forgotten.

"Mark, is that you?"

"Did you think it was a burglar?"

She stood in the kitchen door, tongue-tied at the sight of him. His movements were very deliberate as he removed his coat and flung it down on to the nearest chair. She wondered if he had had anything to eat, and what he had been doing, and she wished more than anything that she had been there doing it with him.

"Shall I cook you something?" she offered, coming a step or two into the kitchen.

"In that?" He made a comprehensive gesture towards her nightwear. "Haven't you eaten yet?"

"It was a long time ago," she murmured. "I could scramble some eggs – or make you an omelette, if you like?"

He sat heavily, not looking at her. "I'd like some coffee," he said.

She made it quickly, hoping that her brew would be to his taste. As an American, he probably thought her own British ideas of what coffee should be too wishy-washy, so, with a touch of recklessness, she added a couple more spoonfuls of coffee to the percolator and plugged it in. She put out two cups on the table, then sat down opposite him, waiting for the coffee to be ready.

It was he, however, who poured the coffee, pushing one of the cups towards her with a slight smile. "You shouldn't have waited up for me," he told her. "I'm not accustomed to having all my needs catered for in this way."

She blinked. "I could still cook you something. I mean – if you haven't everything you want –" She broke off. "If you're hungry?"

He put the coffee pot down and came round behind her. "From your point of view that was an unfortunate way of putting things," he mocked her. "But since you ask, no, I haven't everything I want. And if you don't like it, my little beauty, you shouldn't have come down here trailing clouds of glory and putting ideas in my head!" He grasped her by the arm and drew her upwards towards him, pressing his mouth down on her own. His searching hands pulled her closer still, exploring her hips and the soft curve of her breasts.

She had no defence against him. Her arms went up round his neck and she hid her face in his neck. "Oh, Mark," she whispered, "it's terribly late –"

"I didn't ask you down here. You shouldn't have given me such a warm welcome when I'm as tired as I am at this minute!"

"I'm not surprised you're tired!" She swallowed, looking at him accusingly. "I suppose you've been – *dancing*!"

"Why not?" he confirmed. "Dancing girls are more generous than the Ursulas of this world. They give pleasure as much for the joy of it as for money. How about you, Melâhat?

Would you like to dance for me and have your traditional reward?"

"I don't know," she said. She pulled away from him, suddenly afraid of where they were going, and very much aware of his eyes on her neckline that was quite revealing enough to her way of thinking. But his strength was greater than hers and he mercilessly commanded her compliance as he kissed her mouth, her eyes, and lowered his lips to her bare shoulders. Then, as suddenly, he put her away from him, forcing her back on to the chair in front of her rapidly cooling cup of coffee.

"There's a lot to be said for the Ottoman custom of owning one's women body and soul, without having to care about tomorrow's consequences," he said dryly. His hands shook as he reached out for his cup and he swallowed down the coffee. Otherwise he was as much in command of himself as ever.

"I – I'm sorry," she said.

"Why? Because I want you and know you want me?"

She blushed. "No. Because you're not Maruk Bey and can't have what you want –"

He turned and looked at her, his grey eyes full of harsh, angry laughter. "Ever the romantic! Go to bed, Madeleine, before I forget you're not Melâhat and take you into my bed. I'm in the mood to forget everything except that you are beautiful and that Ursula makes a most inadequate chaperone –"

"Mark, please don't!"

He looked enquiringly at her. "Do I frighten you?"

"A little, but I don't mind that. But I have got a mind as well as a body –"

"My dear Madeleine, go to bed!"

She stood up shakily. "I'm sorry," she said again.

He flung the dregs of his coffee into the sink and poured himself out a second cup. "Don't be," he said wearily. "You're quite right. When you love someone, you want to share your mind as well as your body with your beloved – and you end up married to them!" He glanced sideways at her. "Can't you see that, at the moment, I don't care a rap about your mind, or care whether you have one at all?"

She gave him a scared glance, her face white and anxious. "Are you hungry?" she asked, painfully changing the subject. "I think you ought to have something to eat."

He shrugged his shoulders. "So fix it for me," he said rudely. "But don't expect any thanks. The way to my heart is not through my stomach!"

She put the frying pan on to heat in silence, breaking a couple of eggs into it and laying out two rashers of bacon in the sizzling heat.

"I like my eggs sunny side up," he told her, "and not too hard."

She found a plate and heated it under the tap, serving the cooked food neatly and putting it in front of him. It looked tempting and she hesitated before turning off the heat, wondering if she would cook another lot for herself.

"Well, go on!" he jeered at her. "You look about the right age for a midnight feast in that get-up!"

She smiled kindly at him. "It's long after midnight. I may as well wait for breakfast. Would you like some toast?"

He caught her hand in his and drew her close beside him. "Madeleine, if I kiss you once more, will you *then* go up to bed?"

She couldn't find any words to answer. Her eyes widened and her heart pounded against his restraining hand. She made no attempt to move, but stood submissively waiting for him either to release her or to make good his threat. When the kiss came, it was as soft as falling snow on her face. "Melâhat darling, I don't want to hurt you, and I could quite easily, couldn't I?"

She kissed him back warmly on the cheek and then full on the lips. "I'm not afraid," she said.

His arms tightened about her. "You should be! You're too

101

succulent a piece to go gadding about clad only in a wisp of nylon and romantic dreams of what love is like!" He kissed her hard, hurting her mouth. "You might find the reality not at all to your taste."

Her hands grasped his shoulders as she struggled against the weakness in her knees, seeking the remnants of a self-possession that had long since departed in the face of his caress. "Mark, do you think I can be in love with you?" she asked him tearfully.

His arms dropped to his side and he shook his head slowly at her. "I'd say you were in love with your own romantic dreams. Goodnight, sweetheart. Thanks for the late-night meal."

She gave him a beseeching look, but there was no gainsaying the granite expression on his face. He was not going to give way. She turned, drooping a little, and went out of the kitchen, slowly mounting the stairs to her room. He came and stood at the foot of the staircase, the light streaming out from the kitchen behind him. She saw, with a twinge of half-scared excitement, that the mockery was well and truly back in his smile.

"Oh, and Madeleine," he drawled, "in case you wondered, I think you have a lovely mind!"

She turned on him, almost falling down the stairs in her urgency. "No, you don't!" she flared at him. "You don't care what I think or feel, or even if I do! You think of women as possessions – just as if you really were Maruk Bey – and not very valuable possessions at that!"

"Bravo!" he cheered. He bowed to her in the Moslem fashion, touching first his heart and then his forehead. "Is it not written that *Men stand superior to women in that God has preferred some of them over others*? And that, *Your women are your tilth, so come into your tillage how you choose*? Run, Madeleine, while you still have the chance!"

She gave a shocked, outraged gasp and fled up the stairs,

102

almost knocking Ursula over.

"What on earth are you two doing?" that lady demanded. Her eyes slid over Madeleine's brief nightwear and on to Mark still standing at the foot of the stairs. "I gather it's been an unsuccessful evening all round! Shall we *all* go to bed — our *own* beds?"

Madeleine waited for no further invitation. She scampered up the remaining stairs and, for the first time since coming to the house, she locked the bedroom door securely behind her. Whatever had induced her to go downstairs in the first place? She should have made it clear that she disliked the cheap way he had looked at her, and yet, far from disliking him for it, she had encouraged him to think that she wanted his attentions. He had kissed Ursula the day before, she was practically certain, and who knew how many belly-dancers that evening, and yet she had still gone running into his arms, overjoyed to take her turn in the queue. She must be mad! More than mad, had she no pride? She sat on the edge of her protesting bed and covered her burning cheeks with her hands, facing the unpalatable truth that stared her in the face. She was not mad, unless love was a kind of madness, for, whatever he had said he believed, she knew better. She was deeply, gloriously, irrevocably, in love with him! He had only to lift a finger and she would follow him gladly across the whole face of the earth, no matter what he did to her. And this when she had only known him five minutes! What was it going to be like when she had known him longer and there was no longer any excuse for her not to go back to London? What on earth was she going to do?

"What's the matter with you?"

Madeleine started, surprised that Ursula should have noticed her increasing difficulty in concentrating on what the older woman was saying. "What did you say?" she asked.

"I said have you seen Mark this morning? He isn't proving

himself to be much of a host, is he? I've hardly set eyes on the man since I got here!"

"He's busy," Madeleine said. "He's writing a thesis on the Ottoman architect Sinan."

"Oh?" Ursula paused for an instant in her prowl round the sitting-room. "Any use to us?"

"I don't think so. I don't think Mark wants to offer it to any magazine. He plans to have it published as a book without selling any of the other rights to anyone."

"You seem to know a lot about it!" Ursula's blue eyes looked thoughtful. "Will he make any money out of it?"

Madeleine shrugged. "I don't think he's interested in the money side."

"You could be right there! Mark has an unnatural indifference to making any real money. That's why I chose Bob in the first place. But Mark has other attributes. If he had the right person behind him, he could make a million dollars without even trying. He has brains in his head, and he knows all the right people. In the States, he commands a lot of respect. It's odd, isn't it? I've never quite been able to understand why, because he's never *done* anything important. He's never even had a particularly important job!"

Madeleine bristled, but she knew better than to defend Mark too obviously. "What did he do? Before he came here, I mean?"

Ursula frowned as if the memory of her brother-in-law's activities displeased her. "He taught in some university – I forget which one. Bob and I hardly ever saw him after our marriage. It was – awkward."

"Oh?" Madeleine watched Ursula as she fingered the brass ash-tray Mark kept on his desk. "Why?"

"There was such rivalry between the two brothers. It was ridiculous, as I kept pointing out to them, but they had been brought up to believe that hard work and a good life was everything – spiced by competition of course, to make the race worthwhile. Mark always did better than Bob. His academic record was better and he played football for his college, which Bob never did! When I got to know them, their father had just died and the two of them were carrying on the business together. It was obvious that it would never work out –"

"And Bob was the elder and therefore prevailed?" Madeleine suggested.

"He was the elder, yes. But he would have gone on letting Mark run rings round him if I hadn't stepped in and put a stop to it."

"I'm surprised Mark allowed you to," Madeleine said.

Ursula looked surprised. "But he was in love with me! They *both* were! It was exciting, as you can imagine, for me to have two beaux from the same family. And such eligible ones! My family was absolutely delighted!" She broke off, a smile playing round her lips. "I *couldn't* make up my mind between them! I didn't really want to, because it was fun having the two of them take me out, and give me perfume and candy until it was coming out of my ears. I could have gone on like that for ever, but my father wasn't having it. He told me I had two weeks in which to make up my mind, otherwise he was sending me off on an extended tour of Europe to forget the two of them. It was quite a moment! I knew he was right, but I wanted both of them. Mark was better fun and just a little bit ruthless, but Bob was more devoted on the whole, and he didn't insist on always having his own way. I chose him in the end because I knew I could make him into something. And I did."

Madeleine was scarcely listening. "Did Mark ask you to marry him?" she asked. If he had done so, she thought, he must have been very much in love with his brother's wife.

Ursula's head snapped round to look at Madeleine. "Why do you ask that?" she demanded. "Have you discussed me with him?"

Madeleine shook her head. "Mark doesn't discuss things like that," she said dryly. "He and the clam have a great deal

105

in common, at least as far as I'm concerned!"

She thought Ursula looked relieved. "No. I suppose not. He wouldn't talk to *everyone* about the things closest to him." She began to prowl round the room again. "I've always thought," she began to speak again, in a high, brittle voice that was meant to hide any emotion she might have been feeling, "that if a girl has decided not to accept a proposal, it's far better to make it clear from the outset, so that it doesn't come to actual words. I told Mark that I was going to marry Bob, and that was that!"

"Poor Mark!"

"Oh, that wasn't the end of the matter! Bob and I still had to cope with him in Adeney Publications. He opposed every move we made. It was spite, of course. He couldn't believe that Bob had taken something from him for a change, instead of the other way about. And the gossip was quite frightful! Mark was written about in every gossip column around, and never with the same woman twice! Bob said it was to show me that he didn't care that I'd turned him down. The two of them began to quarrel about policy too. Bob had come round to my way of thinking that we had to expand or die. It was obvious that we couldn't go on as Mr. Adeney had wanted when he was alive. We'd have got nowhere! We'd grown out of small state stories —"

"I can't imagine Mark preferring the parochial," Madeleine put in quietly.

"Not exactly that," Ursula admitted. "But he wouldn't go along with us when we wanted to get involved in national politics. He thought the idea of Bob going into politics eventually to be laughable!"

"Did he say so?"

"My dear, he shouted it at every meeting we had! It was intolerable! Bob became very angry, largely because he thought Mark was getting at him, and he said that one of them would have to give up his interest in the family business. I

106

went to see Mark and asked him if he would sell out his shares to me." She preened herself unconsciously. "He never could deny me if I really wanted anything, and he sold me the lot without a murmur. He told me he was glad to be rid of them!"

She was silent for so long that Madeleine was afraid that she wasn't going to say any more. Then, as suddenly as she had stopped, Ursula started speaking again.

"I didn't see much of him after that. I didn't think it was fair, because I knew he was still in love with me. Bob saw him once, on his own, and he said Mark blamed me for pushing him out of Adeny Publications and that, if Bob were wise, he'd make his own decisions and not allow me to push him around. That was another piece of spite, if you like! Even Bob could see that. He was always telling me that our expansion depended on me because I went all out for success and so it always came my way. Poor Bob! He worked terribly hard at first to keep up. Then, just as we were really beginning to be successful, he began to say that we had no life of our own at all and that he was sick of it. It was a passing mood, I knew that, and we couldn't afford for me to pay too much attention to his grousing. There was so much to do! There was all the entertaining to do, and I had to do every bit of that! Bob would have invited all his old friends to everything and they didn't begin to mix with the kind of people we were getting to know then."

"What was Mark doing?" Madeleine wanted to know.

"He got himself a job teaching. He's a fully trained architect. First of all he majored in the Fine Arts, or something like that. It wasn't very interesting, but it would have been a useful background for Adeney Publications if he'd cared to make use of it. This time I'll see that he does!"

Madeleine picked up some of the magazines that Mark kept stacked in the bookshelves and turned over the pages, not really looking at them at all. "He reads the magazines. He must be interested to do that."

Ursula smiled wryly. "He keeps writing letters telling us that we've got some obscure fact wrong, if that's what you mean by interest!"

Madeleine laughed, stopping abruptly when she saw the anger on Ursula's face. "I do!" she gulped.

"You wouldn't think it funny if you were in charge of the business! It maddened Bob. It was after one of Mark's letters that he said he couldn't go on as we were any longer." Ursula's mouth trembled at the memory. "He said he had to get away and think things out for himself. He said we lacked vision! Oh, I argued with him. We were going straight for the top! This was the last time for him to have doubts about everything we were doing together! But Bob never had much confidence in himself. He banged out of the house in a furious temper, saying that he would get a permit to cover the Viet-Nam war, and that I could run things just as well without him until he got back. He was killed a couple of months after getting there."

"How awful for you!" Madeleine exclaimed.

Ursula shrugged. "It could have been worse. I'm thankful to say that as I'd already been carrying most of the responsibility of the magazine group, *that* didn't die with him. But it wasn't easy on my own. It was one thing when I had a man behind me, even if I was making most of the real decisions, but when I was on my own, a whole lot of people didn't like it. There are always the few who won't work for a woman, and those who will but expect her to overlook everything but the most glaring failings. That's why I need Mark. And that's why I intend to have him!"

Madeleine watched her fidgeting with Mark's possessions as she talked, and felt sorry for her. She suspected that Ursula had had more to do with her husband's decision to go to Viet-Nam than she was letting on and that knowledge alone must have cast a shadow over everything she had achieved.

Ursula picked up a string of beads, that could have been worry-beads such as many men in Turkey and Greece like to play with in their fingers. She let them glide through her fingers several times in silence, then she lifted them to her nose and smelt them delicately.

"I wonder what fair charmer gave him these!" she burst out angrily. "It's disgusting the way he carries on! If we weren't here, he'd probably bring them right home with him!"

Madeleine almost dropped the magazine she was holding. It was only too likely, she thought, that he would do exactly that! "Perhaps we shouldn't be here," she managed to say. "I don't see why he shouldn't live any way he chooses. I'd hate to think we were in his way."

Ursula gave her a glacial look. "I don't think that's for you to say! I am his sister-in-law. Surely he doesn't expect me to go to a hotel when he has plenty of room for us here?"

"He didn't ask to have us," Madeleine insisted. She hated to think of Mark having anyone else in his house, but neither did she relish the role of preventing him from living as he wished in his own house.

"No," Ursula agreed. She smiled slowly, looking very much more cheerful. "I think he was afraid to ask me here. I really begin to think I've got him cornered! We'll see him back in New York before we know it!"

Madeleine hoped not, but she couldn't help thinking that Ursula was very likely right. Adeney Publications had once meant a great deal to him, and it could do again. It was silly of her to want him to stand out against Ursula's blandishments, if that was what he really wanted to do.

Madeleine helped Mihrimar with the washing up after lunch. The Turkish woman had taken to wearing a rope of blue beads round her head, which she waved in Ursula's direction whenever she saw her. Madeleine suspected that because they were blue, Mihrimar thought they had magical properties and would keep the evil eye away, and she was careful not to mention the matter to Ursula, much as she longed to talk over the local superstitions with someone – preferably with Mark. But of Mark there was no sign.

He came in though for a few minutes in the middle of the afternoon. Ursula had gone up to her room to give herself a leisurely manicure, and Madeleine was on her own in the sitting room. She looked up from her book and saw him, standing in the doorway, quietly studying her.

"*Oh!*" she gasped.

"You look deliciously idle," he said. "Haven't you got anything to do?" He sounded impatient and faintly scornful.

"No," she said.

"Then you can do some typing for me. You can't build your whole life on dreams. Here, you can transcribe these notes and put them in some kind of order. When you've finished them, you can ask me for some more."

"If you're here to ask!"

He looked at her for a long moment. The forbidding expression on his face sent the colour rushing up into her cheeks. She made an uncomfortable movement towards the typewriter and banged it down on to the desk, opening it with a snap.

"I'll call in from time to time," he said smoothly.

"Mrs. Adeney is upstairs," she told him, rigidly polite because he looked tired and she thought he might well have a hangover.

"I'll see her tomorrow," he answered. "Will you tell her and Mihrimar that I shall be out to dinner. It's a long-standing engagement that I can't very well get out of."

Madeleine nodded, aware only of her own bitter disappointment that he was going out again.

"And don't let me catch you sitting around doing nothing again!" he added. "If you want a credit for typing my thesis, you'll have to earn it." He smiled suddenly, patting her on the shoulder. "Besides, it's about the only thing that will keep Ursula out of your hair! She'll yell blue murder when she finds she's on her own again tonight!"

CHAPTER VIII

MADELEINE worked on Mark's notes as though her life depended on it. In a way it did. Ursula's influence spread itself throughout the house, so that it was hard to remember what it had been like before her coming. A clutter of feminine odds and ends, all of them belonging to Ursula, took possession of the sitting room as if by right and even the dining room had its share of women's magazines and scented writing paper scattered over the sideboard and table. Madeleine would feel herself going rigid with sheer rage when she discovered another pair of nylons, or a cardigan, or even a pair of elegant suede gloves, bundled under a cushion in one of the easy chairs. Mark, on the other hand, showed no sign of noticing the way his home was being invaded. He came and went as he pleased, avoiding all arguments with a skill that Madeleine could only admire and envy. To her, he hardly spoke at all.

Sometimes, Madeleine suspected, he and Ursula would wait until she had gone to bed and would talk to one another then. She could only judge the results from Ursula's moods the next morning, from which she gathered that although Ursula would go as far as she dared in furthering her campaign to get her brother-in-law to bend to her will, she was not being wholly successful. There were days when Madeleine too could feel Mark's appreciation of Ursula's physical attributes and knew a burning sense of jealousy that frightened her by its intensity. But more often Ursula would appear for breakfast, a sullen rage brooding behind her eyes, telling its own story that Mark had still not agreed to return to the United States with her.

On Friday, the day began particularly badly. Madeleine

111

had delayed going downstairs until after she had stripped the beds ready for Mihrimar to take the sheets away to be washed, so Ursula was already pouring out her coffee at the table when she went into the dining room. Madeleine sat down opposite her and glared at the crisp warm rolls in front of her with a total lack of appetite.

"Coffee?" Ursula asked her. Her voice sounded funny and Madeleine looked at her suspiciously. She was surprised to see that Ursula was trying not to cry and that her eyes were already shadowed by the tears she had shed.

"Has something happened?"

"No," Ursula said in muffled tones. "That's the trouble! I'm not getting anywhere, and I can't bear it! He doesn't understand that I need him! I'd do anything to get him to come back into my life. I can't go on alone – I can't! And he doesn't even care!"

Madeleine found herself wondering how genuine were the tears and the apparent despair, and promptly took herself to task for her lack of sympathy. She searched helplessly for some words of comfort, but found none that would have sounded remotely sincere. Ursula, however, seemed not to have noticed her silence.

"Why else does he suppose I came to Turkey? I had to see him again! If he would only come back, things would be different, but he doesn't believe me!"

"You didn't go to Ankara to find him," Madeleine pointed out.

Ursula blinked. "What has that got to do with it? Anyway, that was quite different!" She coloured delicately, looking suddenly younger. "I heard that a friend of mine was in Ankara. He's a friend of long standing and I wanted so badly to see him! He's in Nato, you know. I'm very fond of him. He – he wants to marry me, as a matter of fact, only he won't put up with a working wife because he's abroad so much. He says I must sell Adeney Publications." Her lips took on a mutinous

112

slant. "I won't, though. We're making money at last, real money, and I meet everyone who is anyone and they're interested in what I have to say. They wouldn't be interested in *me* if I were only the wife of an army officer! He wants too much, so I told him! I'll never sell Adeney Publications. It's mine and that's the way it's going to stay! Not even Mark can take that away from me, though I suppose I shall have to give him an impressive title to keep him sweet. But the real power will always be mine!"

Madeleine's sympathy died still-born. Was that all she was offering Mark? A high-sounding title to give him a spurious status, while she kept everything that mattered in her own greedy hands? Didn't she know that Mark would never be content with that? That he would never stand for being the prop beneath a woman's throne, no matter who the woman. He would expect a public abdication at the very least, signed and sealed with love. But Ursula had no love to offer him. Her only care was how she could make use of him, how best to bend him to her whim. It was a sickening display of selfishness.

"Mark will never agree to taking second place," she said aloud.

"He'll never know! I know just how to feed his ego. He's not so very different from his brother!"

It was a depressing thought. Madeleine tried to tell herself that Mark would never give way to Ursula's ambitions, but she knew how convincing the American girl could be when she wanted to be. Mark might well think that he owed it to his dead brother to take his place in the family business, and then Ursula would have won and Mark would have lost his hard-won independence.

Work failed to assuage the anger which the exchange with Ursula had roused within her. Madeleine pounded the type-writer for an hour or more, knowing that she would have to do much of the work all over again, but using the noise she was making as a cover behind which she could retreat from any further conversation. It was only when she went to help Mihrimar hang out the wet sheets to dry that she realised that Ursula seemed to be just as intent on avoiding her. Mihrimar managed to tell her in the mixture of signs and basic words with which they conversed that Ursula intended to have her lunch in bed. Madeleine could hardly keep the joy out of her face and voice as she came in from the garden.

"I'm going out!" she called up the stairs to Ursula. There was no answer. "Mrs. Adeney?"

"Go where you like!"

Madeleine didn't wait for her to change her mind. She grabbed her coat and bag from the hall and rushed out of the house, doubly glad that the sun was shining and that she was out in it.

On the ferry, she began to consider what she was going to do with her few hours of freedom. Her work on Mark's notes made her think that she would like to see for herself that crowning achievement of Sinan's work, the Süleymaniye, a monument to his master Suleiman the Magnificent, containing the mausoleums of both sultan and architect, together with that of Roxelana, as well as the largest mosque in the city, and all the other buildings that go to make up the complex: the school, the public kitchens, and so on.

Madeleine thought that she would walk up from the Galata Bridge to the imposing building on the skyline, but it wasn't as easy to find her way as she had thought. She came to another mosque on the way, in front of which a crowd of people were feeding the pigeons, hoping to gain merit from the action. Madeleine stopped and asked an old woman who was selling corn to the passers by which way she should go. "Süleymaniye?" she asked.

Astonished that she should have been asked, the old lady cackled with glee, and pointed down a turning that led alongside the rear of the Istanbul University buildings. Madeleine set out at a good pace, but became increasingly uncertain as she went on. Then, just as she was about to ask again, she saw the minarets and the huge dome of the mosque in front of her and hurried to cross the road, almost getting herself run over in the process.

A traffic policeman admonished her gravely, and saw her personally across the road, saluting her as she stepped safely on to the pavement. Madeleine found herself standing by a small restaurant and her thoughts began to turn towards food. Through the glass door she could see the gigantic bowls of different foods put out to tempt the appetite of the patrons. There was also a price-list, which meant little enough to her because she had no idea what most of the dishes were called. Seeing her hesitate, the owner opened the door for her and waved her inside, his delighted smile warming her. She had thought he might not like to have an unaccompanied woman in his restaurant, but he seemed only too pleased. He pointed to the various dishes, drawing her attention to the charcoal fire over which small pieces of meat were being roasted.

"Yes, that!" she agreed, her mouth watering at the smell of the cooking meat.

He nodded his head enthusiastically. "Salad, yes?" he went on in the few words of English he had at his disposal. "Bread?"

She agreed to both these extras and sat down rather gingerly by the window in the place he had cleared for her. There was American cloth on all the tables and nothing to sit on but the cheapest kind of wooden stool, but the atmosphere was friendly. Several young people were eating at the next-door table. They looked like university students, which made her think that she had come to the right place if it was well patronised by the local people. The owner of the restaurant wiped the cloth in front of her and poured her out a glass of ice-cold water as a matter of course, smiling down at her.

"American? English?" he asked her.

"English," she said. Her eyes met those of the traffic policeman outside and she smiled at him. He bowed politely and made a mime of eating well that amused her. She felt as though a great weight had been lifted off her shoulders and knew that it was no more than that she had got away from Ursula for a few hours and that she was enjoying herself.

The proprietor came back with her plate of meat and rice, carrying a mixed salad of lettuce, onions, peppers and sliced tomatoes in his other hand. He whisked up a table-napkin, still wet from being washed, and placed it on her knee, returning a second later with an enormous slab of bread and some clean cutlery. When he had assured himself that Madeleine had everything she wanted, he stood for a moment, looking out of the window. Then apparently he saw someone he knew, for, waving his arms in the air to attract attention, he went flying out of the restaurant, his laughter ringing down the street.

Madeleine didn't wish to seem curious, so she turned her attention to her meal, picking up the heavy fork and attacking the lacy-edged lettuce that looked so appetising. She had barely done so when somebody sat down beside her. She turned hastily, her jumping heart telling her who it was before she had looked at him. He smiled slowly, but just as he was about to speak, the restaurant owner came rushing forward, shaking him warmly by the hand. Madeleine couldn't understand a word of what they said to one another, but here too he seemed to be known as Maruk Bey, and was every bit as popular as he had been at the Topkapi Palace.

"What are you doing out alone?" He turned to her at last, his light-grey eyes resting thoughtfully on her face.

"Why shouldn't I go out?" she retorted. "I've been in all week!"

"I said, what are you doing alone?" he repeated.

She didn't know how to answer. "Ursula was – upset," she said at last. "She went to her room."

"I see." She wondered if he did, not that she could have explained to him the joy of being free of Ursula's presence for

116

a while. "Aren't you afraid you might be picked up by some man with an eye for a pretty face?"

She looked mischievously up at him. "Oh, Mark, will you? I'm going to look at the Suleiman mosque."

"Any particular reason for your choice?"

"Of course." She was able to quote from his own notes. "'There can be few centres that can compare with the Süleymaniye, in its extent, in the grandeur of its conception, in the ingenuity of the work, or in the harmony of the various parts that make up the whole.' I want to see this marvel for myself. Besides," she added, "I've become interested in Sinan's works."

"Then see it you shall!" He received his own meal from the proprietor and poured himself some water. "I'll take you to the Islamic Museum while we're about it. It's housed in the old kitchens of the mosque."

Madeleine thanked him. "Why are there kitchens attached to all the old mosques?" she asked. "Were they monasteries as well?"

"Some of them," he answered. "Islam demands very high standards of hospitality. Before the State took over such functions, anyone could claim a hot meal from the public kitchens of any mosque. You still can at a few of them. At Eyüp, for example."

"Just like the medieval monasteries."

She had finished her meat before Mark, but she was happy to sit and watch him eat his. It seemed a long time since she had shared a meal with him, and she was aware of a feeling of guilt all over again that she and Ursula should have driven him out of his own house.

"How long is Mrs. Adeney staying with you?" she asked as he put down his knife and fork.

"Long enough! Shall I order you some yoghourt to finish with, or would you like to try something more exotic?"

"I don't know what the other things are," she said.

117

"Some of them are worth trying." His eyes filled with sudden amusement. "They have exotic names like 'woman's thigh' or 'woman's navel', but I don't know that I'd recommend many of them. How about *baklava*? It's layers of thin pastry with ground walnuts and syrup. A piece of that won't take up much room and you can still have some yoghourt to finish up with."

She accepted his advice, wondering if she would have enough money to pay for all these delicacies. She fingered the one hundred-lire note that he himself had given her and tried to work out in her mind what the meal had already cost her. "Is it expensive?" she asked hesitantly.

"Why, are you short?"

"N—no, not exactly. Only I think Mrs. Adeney thinks the London office is paying me while I'm here."

"And they're not?"

She shook her head. "I have a little money of my own, though," she assured him. "And I haven't had the opportunity to spend much anyway!"

The glint in his eyes told her that he, too, knew she had *some* money. She hoped that he wouldn't guess that apart from that single note she had only the remains of the three pounds' worth of lire that she had been allowed by her bank in England. He gave her a teasing glance that brought the colour to her cheeks.

"Then it's just as well you allow yourself to be picked up by strange men, my sweet. You can hardly be expected to pay for your own meal under the circumstances!"

She wriggled uncomfortably on her wooden stool. "No, I want to! It isn't fair that you should have to pay for me. It's bad enough —" She broke off, realising that there were some things that were better left unsaid.

"Yes?" The severity of that bleak syllable made her heart jerk within her.

"You can't want to have us in your house!" she said evasively.

"That's not your worry, Melâhat. How's the typing going?"

She told him that she had nearly finished the pile he had given her. "I wouldn't have come out today, but I can do the last of it this evening, and I did want to see Sinan's most famous creation for myself." She smiled happily at him. "It will be marvellous to have you show it to me! That makes it perfect!"

"You're easily pleased!" he drawled.

But she shook her head, looking at him through her eyelashes and smiling. "I'm easily disappointed. You will show me *everything*, won't you?"

"I'll do my best," he promised with a mocking indulgence that set her blood racing. How foolish she had been to think that she could ever do anything but love him, she thought. She had been even more foolish to think that time had anything to do with it! One look had been enough, no matter how often she had denied it to herself. "We'd better get going!" he went on dryly. "So you can take that dreamy expression off your face, my girl, and pay attention to the master! He may be dead, but he still has a great deal to say to the living!"

Madeleine produced her hundred-lire note, but he waved it away, paying for both their lunches with a firmness that made any further argument pointless. He shook hands with the restaurant owner, smoothly pushing Madeleine out of the door before him. Out in the street, he took her hand in his and pulled her across the street to the evident amusement of the traffic policeman. Madeleine confessed blithely that she had nearly been run over in just that spot and had been rescued by the policeman, and how nice he had been to her.

"You're not safe to be allowed out on your own!" Mark rebuked her. "It's more than time that someone kept you in their eye!"

Madeleine chuckled. "*Gözde*?" she suggested. "I knew we'd

get back to my natural inferiority as a woman!" It gave her a delightful, breathless feeling to be flirting with him. "I can look after myself, you know."

"To be *gözde* is all right," he observed, "but it's time you graduated to the next stage of being *ikbal*, or successful, don't you think?"

She averted her face, glad that he couldn't possibly know how easily she would settle for being anything as far as he was concerned. "Why now?" she asked.

"You think it too soon?" His nonchalance smote her like a blow on the face. "One can talk nonsense at any time, Melâhat, and not mean anything by it," he added more gently. "When it ceases to be nonsense, I won't leave you in any doubt about it. Will that do for now?"

She nodded without speaking. He had told her plainly enough that he expected to take the initiative in any relationship he chose to have with a woman. Always and for ever! Her part would only be to follow his lead. She thought of him standing at the foot of the stairs and saying, *Is it not written* –? Only Ursula would stand out against him. She wouldn't care if it were 'written' or not! All she cared about was her own convenience and making him do as she wished. Madeleine envied Ursula her confidence. She herself knew that she stood no chance of moving him from his chosen course, even supposing that she had wanted to, but Ursula's weapons were those of family and power. Such weapons might well prevail.

"I was talking nonsense too!" she said lightly, releasing her hand from his hold and hurrying ahead of him across the courtyard that fronted the mosque.

"Naturally so," he drawled. "Since you affect to believe that women are men's equals in every way, to be some man's favourite would be a sad comedown!"

She lifted her chin, too proud to show that he had hurt her. "To govern well you need the consent of those you rule," she admonished him. "That's the hard part!"

He was remarkably unimpressed. "Democracy is a long way from the harem," he said. "Still, I'll bear it in mind the next time I want to kiss you!"

Her eyelids flickered nervously. It wasn't fair! In any argument between them he would always win hands down. They both knew that physically he could dominate her any time he chose. If he stopped to ask her, the result would be just the same: he would demand and she would submit and would delight in her own weakness. You could call it chemistry, or the way that things were meant to be, but she wouldn't like it at all if it were the other way about!

Mark turned his back on her, his interest fully on the courtyard in which they were standing. "They say the four minarets denote that Suleiman was the fourth sultan to rule in Istanbul and the ten balconies that he was the tenth sultan of the Osman line. I don't know about the truth of that, but only an imperial mosque may have as many minarets. I believe that the Blue Mosque is the only one in the world to have six minarets. They say that in that case the young sultan asked for them to be built of gold, to the architect's despair. He came up with the answer of having six minarets and pretending that's what he had thought the sultan had commanded. The Turkish words for six and gold are rather similar."

Madeleine spent a long time looking at the minarets. It seemed impossible to her that any man could climb up the circular staircase inside to call the faithful to prayer. He would have to be a dwarf!

"They do, you know," Mark said. "Though not often these days. Nowadays they have a microphone at ground level. In some places they use a record, but that's forbidden in Istanbul."

He went across to the entrance of the mosque, taking off his shoes with the ease of long practice. He stood in his stockinged feet, watching critically as she followed his example. "When they pray," he said, "their heads come in contact with the carpets, so they like to keep them clean."

Madeleine thought it added a touch of the exotic to their entrance. She waited while Mark folded back the heavy leather curtain that covered the open door for her to precede him into the vast prayer hall of the mosque. The severe grandeur of the interior brought her to a standstill. The stained glass, quite as pretty as that in the Topkapi harem, added a touch of colour to the eastern wall, highlighting the *mihrab*, the niche that points directly towards Mecca. Above, covering the vast empty room below, was the huge dome, decorated with writings from the Koran written in the ancient Turkish script. Otherwise there was no furniture to detract from the feeling of space, only the magnificent carpet on the floor and the hanging lights, kept low over the worshippers.

Mark spent some time explaining to her how Sinan had solved the problems presented to him by having such a vast dome. He showed her how, on the north and south sides, he had incorporated the buttresses into the walls of the building, masking them with galleries, and on the east and west sides the buttresses were smaller for the weight of the dome was distributed by means of semi-domes. But Madeleine's interest lay in the windows and the discreetly used colours, some of the earliest known examples from the famous Iznik kilns, in turquoise, deep blue and red.

"The windows are lovely from the door, but they're hard to see when one gets up to them," she remarked.

"That's because they're set in at an angle," he answered. He grinned at her. "The glazier was known as Sarhos Ibrahim, Sarhos meaning the Drunkard!"

Madeleine was disappointed. For some reason she had pictured Sinan building the mosque with his own hands, and she didn't like any of the credit for its beauty to go elsewhere. "What about the carpet?" she asked.

Mark's enthusiasm kindled hers and she readily became ecstatic at the sheer size of the carpet that spread from one wall to the other. "You remember how some prayer carpets are made for whole families to pray together?" he reminded her. "Well, this is the gallery prayer carpet par excellence! Each square delineates the space allotted to one man. Look, these stylised footprints are to show him where to put his feet, and here is the narrowing of the design that shows the direction of Mecca!"

She fitted her own feet on to the footprints, surprised at the amount of space she had to herself. Beside her, Mark did likewise, showing her the various attitudes of prayer, beginning by putting his hands on his knees, then kneeling down, then finally prostrating himself with his forehead on the carpet.

"Do women do that too?" she asked him.

"Not in public! They may do in the privacy of their own homes, but I wouldn't know about that!"

She raised her eyebrows in disbelief. "No?"

"No, baggage, I do not! I guess the women I know are not the praying sort!" He stood up straight and put his arm round her waist. "Does it come up to your expectations, or are you disappointed in the great Sinan now that you've seen his masterpiece?"

She shook her head, taking a last look at the huge prayer hall all round her. "One would have to be very hard to please to be disappointed in this," she murmured. "It makes one feel rather small in the presence of Allah. I like that."

"I guess that's the idea," he agreed expansively.

She sat on one of the deep steps in the courtyard to replace her shoes, wishing that she could just step into her shoes as he did with his. "Isn't that fountain beautiful?" she said, struggling with a knotted lace. "Is that where they wash before they pray?"

"They used to. It became too small for the numbers who come here, though, so nowadays they wash elsewhere. We'll probably see them as we go out."

But the only person to be washing his arms, feet and head was one very small boy. He had drawn his trousers up to his

123

knees so as not to get them wet, and he found them very much more interesting than what he was doing. Mark wished him a cheerful good day and the child grinned and went back to his ablutions.

"How did you learn to speak Turkish?" Madeleine asked him, annoyed that she too couldn't exchange a few words with the boy.

"Not easily! I had a little Hungarian – I don't know whether that helped or not! But most of all I wanted to speak to the Turks in their own language, and they loved teaching me!"

She could well imagine who his most enthusiastic teachers had been! She took a last look at the courtyard behind them and glanced up at him. "Did you call any of them Melâhat?" she asked deliberately.

"No, my jealous one, I did not!" He leaned towards her, his face very close to hers. "It doesn't become you to fish for compliments!" He was echoing her own words to him. "Do you want to visit the Islamic museum now?"

She nodded, not trusting herself to speak. The look in his eyes disturbed her, but he did no more than flick her cheek with a thoughtful finger, and lead the way round the wall of the mosque to where the old kitchens were situated. A small notice, in both Turkish and English, announced the presence of one of the most valuable collections of Moslem books and relics in the world. Mark wandered through the open door, bought their entrance tickets, and guided her into the first of the rooms. An ancient guardian came into the room after them, turning on the lights, and bidding them look round with a courtly gesture. He came round after them, pointing out the more interesting of the ancient Korans, the stiff script of the ones from Cordova in Spain, the illustrated ones from the Seljuk period, and the later, gloriously illuminated ones from the Ottoman period. Madeleine was astonished to find that most of these priceless books were considerably older than the Doomsday Book and yet, apart from the cases they were in, very little special care seemed to be taken of them.

On one wall were a number of the distinctive signatures of the various sultans, with its three upright bars topping a snail-shaped flourish. The different squiggles that made up the foot of the snail made it possible to tell one monarch's seal from another, but for one who could not read the ancient script, it was easy to mistake one for another.

Madeleine was thoughtful as they passed on to some examples of Turkish carpets, made hundreds of years ago, and some examples of early metalwork and gold and silver jewellery. Mark was looking at some inlaid covers that were used to hold copies of the Koran when travelling, or merely to store them.

"You love these things, don't you?" she said.

He nodded easily. "Imagine the civilisation that made all this beauty possible!" he exclaimed. "In my opinion it was one of the greatest in the world!"

She made a face at him, not sure if she agreed with him or not. "It was all right for the men," she said. "I wouldn't have liked to be a woman — I don't think I'd like to be a Moslem woman now!"

"I don't see why not," he answered. "They have a very definite role in society, and that means they are respected. The man has his public life, but it is the woman who reigns supreme in the home. She has her needs catered for by her husband and that works well. He is the head of the household, but the worries are all his too."

"But supposing she wants to do something in her own right?" Madeleine objected.

"Up to a point, she can. But few want to. Why should she compete in the man's sphere when she still has a fulfilling sphere of her own? If that were taken away from her, as it largely has been in some cultures, then she must do so. But here, her function has remained unchallenged, and she's all the happier for that!"

"*You* may think so –"

"I do. She is sure of herself, not trying to turn herself into an ersatz man and beat him at his own game."

"But she remains his chattel, whatever you say!"

He laughed. "Wouldn't you rather be the chattel of a man than the equal of a mouse?" he mocked her.

Madeleine turned away, feeling herself to be on dangerous ground. "I ought to be going home," she said.

He watched her for a moment as she struggled with her urgent desire to stay and do whatever he was going to do next.

"If you want to understand Islam better, I'll take you to see Eyüp," he offered, putting a hand on her shoulder. "You can go home after that!"

She made no attempt to hide her pleasure. "Eyüp is at the other end of the Golden Horn, isn't it? Oh, yes, please, Mark! May we really go there?"

CHAPTER IX

MARK had no difficulty in finding his way through the twisting, complicated streets back to the Galata Bridge. Madeleine followed on, a little behind him, interested in everything she saw. She wanted to give the old beggar who asked for alms in the name of Allah all the loose coins she had, but Mark hurried her on, frowning at her lack of sophistication.

"My dear girl, he could buy and sell you several times over!" he shot at her. But Madeleine was too contented to rise to his strictures.

"I daresay. Almost anyone could at this moment! But I should have liked to have given him something. I've only ever seen someone begging in the name of Allah on the stage before, and he did look the part! Did you see that splendid cast in his eye?"

"Put on for the occasion!"

Madeleine laughed at his cynicism. "You have no heart!" she sighed.

"You mean I haven't your thirst for seeing romance lurking round every corner! One day cold reality will give you your come-uppance, while you're off chasing your pretty butterflies!" He gave her a slanting smile. "Let's hope there'll be someone around to pick up the pieces. That task might well have its own rewards."

A shadow crossed Madeleine's face. She already knew the exact moment when her life would be shattered, and she knew too that there would be no one around to pick up the pieces. That moment would be when she left Istanbul and went out of Mark's life for ever.

127

She was rescued from the slough of despondency into which she had slithered by their arrival at the Galata Bridge. The sun had disappeared behind some rain clouds, hastening on the early darkness of winter, but the access to the bridge was as crowded as ever. Fish stalls predominated, with others selling breads covered with sesame seeds running them a close second. Black-clad women, toting heavy shopping bags, hurried through the mud that made the roads and pavements slippery and hard to traverse. Their menfolk ran hither and thither, quietly, without fuss, pushing their way through the nose-to-tail cars that thronged the streets, intent on their own destinations.

Naturally Madeleine dawdled further behind as Mark cut his way briskly through the crowds and, naturally, she finally lost sight of him altogether and had a nasty couple of moments anxiously seeking him, only to find him standing by a fish-stall, watching her panic. "Serve you right!" he said unsympathetically as she came up to him. "You'd better hold my hand!"

She was only too willing. "Have you ever seen the bridge when it's open in the early morning?" she asked him.

"Once," he said. "More interesting is that this bridge is the one after which the card game is called. For a long time it was the only bridge across the Golden Horn, and so it was commonly known as 'the bridge', without any other name. It happened that there was an English family living on either side of the bridge and they used to meet most evenings to play a variation of whist that they had invented between them. Neither side much liked crossing the bridge in the evenings, though. They got wet when it rained, and so on, and there was always the risk of being mugged. So they got into the habit of saying to one another, it's your night to bridge tomorrow! And so the game they played came to be known as bridge!"

She was pleased with the story, but her attention soon wandered to the bevy of small boats that bobbed up and down on

128

the inside of the bridge. Now and again one of them would break loose and ply its way up the Golden Horn towards the "Sweet Waters of Europe", as the streams that fed the Horn were called. It was possible to dismiss the pollution of the waters in this light and to see only the pale reflection of the sunset that had given the strip of water its name. Madeleine could imagine what it would be like if the rain were not threatening, with the gold and scarlet of the sunset in the sky burning as vividly in the waters below.

Mark had less time for dreaming. He hurried her through a muddy puddle towards a bus stop and, finding a bus in its last death throes already standing by the side of the road, he shoved her firmly into the crowded interior, ignoring her protests that there was no room to breathe inside, let alone for another body to stand in the area that he intended that she should.

The packed-in passengers adjusted themselves reluctantly to the newcomers. Madeleine, unable to find anything else to hang on to, clung on to Mark's hand, managed to turn to face the front, and was immediately appalled to see that the driver was sharing his seat with no fewer than three young boys, each of them complete with school satchel and triumphant expression at having found somewhere to sit.

Madeleine cast a look round the rest of her fellow passengers, uncomfortably aware that she was standing on somebody's foot. When she found the owner she apologised as well as she could, a trifle dismayed by the hot look in his eyes and the warmth of his smile. It was her imagination, she thought, and tried to dismiss him from her mind. He had no intention of being so easily forgotten, however. He leaned forward a mere half-inch, breathing hard in her face. Then, much to her relief, Mark said something in Turkish, squeezing himself between her and her tormentor. An instant later she found herself hard up against the side of the bus, with Mark's solid frame between her and the rest of the crushed passengers.

For a moment she was too grateful to him to do other than smile her thanks and try to give him room to put his feet. But the compact strength of his frame against the whole length of her body did funny things to her breathing and her heart took on an acrobatic life of its own. He put an arm round her, hanging on to the catch of the broken window, and he grinned at her, his eyes inscrutable.

"That was one bit of romance you could do without," he said just as if the whole incident had been her fault.

She nodded, wondering whether the pounding of her heart was as evident to him as it was to her. She didn't dare look directly at him, but contented herself with studying the collar of his shirt, glad that he didn't mind wearing bright colours and fancy flowered ties. They suited his arrogantly masculine personality, moulding the whipcord muscles of his neck and shoulders, and accentuating the width of his chest and the slimness of his waist.

The bus rumbled into action. If it had been empty, it could not possibly have gone faster than walking pace; laden to bursting point, it went slower still, lurching round the cobbled corners and groaning up and down the hills. Mark changed his hold on to the window catch from one hand to the other, keeping his arm firmly round Madeleine to prevent her from falling. She was almost sure that his lips touched her neck just below her ear, but she was too shy to look up to see. Her heart went into swooping action at the thought, betraying the stillness of her crushed stance. She felt rather than heard his sudden amusement and tried to keep the flood of colour from surging up into her cheeks. That she was not very successful, she could tell from the way his arms tightened about her. His smile, she thought, was triumphantly male and superior, as was the gleam in his eye. "How is it we are either looking for a chaperon, or have an excess of them, my Melâhat?" he asked her.

She strove to maintain her equilibrium, making a play of looking out at the darkening streets behind her. Almost immediately, the bus ground to a halt and Mark had released his hold on the window and was making a path for her to push her way towards the door, to be disgorged on to the pavement just in time for the bus to totter off along the road. Mark stood beside her, looking completely uncrumpled after their experience. He put his head on one side and watched her while she painfully straightened out her cramped limbs and brushed the worst of the creases out of her raincoat.

"If we hurry," he said, "we'll just have time for you to see the outside of the mosque in daylight."

She looked round, expecting to see the place of pilgrimage right beside her, but there was nothing to be seen but narrow, mean streets, made worse by the running mud that was a legacy of the recent rain.

"It was here, in this village, that Pierre Loti sat in his café and soaked up the atmosphere of imperial decline for his novels. You should read him, if you want to know what Istanbul was like before the Young Turks took over."

Madeleine badly wanted to say that she had read his books, but as she was normally truthful and knew that he would know that she had never read a French novel in her whole life, she restrained herself and followed him up the street of his choice instead, coming out into a rather grand square that contrasted favourably with the street where the bus had put them down. The traffic was not as intense as it was in the city and there was an air of peace that spread out towards them, welcoming them into the dusk-bound holy place of Islam.

"*Allahu akbar! La ilaha ill'llah!*" The liquid cry rang out over their heads, the soaring human voice ending in a crescendo of praise. Mark pointed up to the top of the slender minaret and to Madeleine's delight she could just make out the tiny figure of a man on the balcony.

"He doesn't use a microphone!" she exclaimed. "I didn't think one would be able to hear him half so well! He must have a fantastically powerful voice!"

"Perhaps he trains like an opera singer," Mark suggested, and Madeleine giggled. "Shall we go inside?" he added. He glanced at his watch. "I'm afraid we're too late to go inside the *türbe* itself –"

"The *türbe* of Eyüp," she said rolling the words on her tongue. "Who was Eyüp? He must have been frightfully important."

"He was the standard-bearer and friend of the Prophet. The newly converted Arabs laid siege to the city in 669 and Eyüp-ül-Ensari Halit bin Zeyd was one of those who were killed. He was buried on the battlefield, no one quite knew where. Much later, during the seige of Mehmet the Conqueror, the Sultan had a dream which revealed the site of the holy grave. When they searched the place, they found it was true, and a tomb and mosque were built over the site. That mosque was made unsafe by earthquakes and the present one was built in 1800. It was here that the Commander of the Faithful was girded with the Sword of Osman, the symbol of the Caliphate. The faithful come here too on their way to the great pilgrimage to Mecca. And the boys of Istanbul come here on the day of their circumcision, dressed in white, with a scarlet sash, and a white pillbox hat. It's a very great day in their lives."

The mosque shone white in the darkness, extraordinarily clean and well-preserved. It was entered through an irregularly shaped courtyard. Mark said that the ancient plane trees housed lame storks that had found a sanctuary there, and that sometimes these were joined by grey herons who built their nests in the branches in the spring. The pigeons, fat as butter, were always there, quarrelling over the largesse of the many visitors. They were less exciting than the nobler birds, but they added a cheerful charm to the place, strutting up and down between the serious-faced men who were carefully washing themselves before going into the prayer-hall.

The tomb of Eyüp, or Job as he would be called in English, was locked and barred as Mark had feared. A queue of petitioners stood outside the brass latticed window, waiting to make their requests of the long-dead saint. Each one waited his, or her, turn in patient silence. Many of them held their shoes in one hand, ready for the moment when they would go inside to pray.

Madeleine took off her own shoes and followed Mark into the lighted mosque. She had a vivid impression of honey-coloured stone with decorations of gold, a magnificent chandelier hanging from the dome, its stars of light drawing her eyes to the single turquoise carpet, patterned in blue, that covered the floor from wall to wall.

"It was a gift of the late President Menderes," Mark whispered to her, noting where she was looking.

She looked at the carpet again, feeling the depth of the pile with her bare toes. She would have followed Mark further into the hall, but he gestured for her to go into the enclosure at the rear with the rest of the women, disappearing himself into the crowd of prostrate figures under the lights. She hastily obeyed him, finding that she was the only woman to have stepped over the dividing line. She tried sitting on her feet, as the other women did, but they rapidly went to sleep underneath her. How did they sit like that, for hours at a time, without moving at all? She felt as restless as a fidgety child and kneeled up to gain some relief from the pins and needles that pricked her feet and thighs.

Mark was a long time coming back to her. She looked round the prayer-hall, hoping to see him, but there was no sign of him anywhere. For a moment, she was back in her panic when she had lost him at the Galata Bridge, and she stood up quickly, almost running to the door to see if he had gone outside. The courtyard was practically deserted now and almost completely dark. Mark was not there either. She forced herself to be calm, telling herself that he had to be somewhere and would come and find her soon enough. She put on her shoes and trailed round the courtyard, not caring that the rain was wetting her hair and would probably seep through her raincoat as well.

The Window of Help in Eyüp's tomb drew her back across the courtyard. She peered through the lattice work, but it was too dark to see much but a few shadowed, gleaming shapes that could have been anything. She grasped the brass window and shut her eyes tight.

"Oh, Eyüp," she said silently, "I don't know who you were, not really. But help me!" She swallowed, not knowing how to continue. How could she put what she wanted into words? Mark wouldn't change! Yet how much she would have given to be the only woman in his life, to love and be loved by him! "If it's possible," she said to the holy man. "If it's possible, let it be true!"

She felt Mark's hand on her arm and looked round quickly, embarrassed lest he should have read her mind and recognised the fervour of her request.

"Do you always make a wish if the opportunity comes your way?" he asked, looking amused. "Do you turn the silver in your pocket when you see the new moon?"

She cast a surreptitious look up at the sky, but the moon was nowhere to be seen. It would no longer be the crescent shape she had last seen, but would have fattened into something approaching the spherical globe of the full moon.

"I – I couldn't find you anywhere!" she accused.

"You won't lose me easily," he answered. "Shall we go across the square and have some tea?"

She nodded silently. But he made no effort to move. On the contrary, he himself stood in front of the Window of Help, his head bowed, making his own request. But the things he wanted were not what she wanted, she thought miserably. He would want to be rid of both herself and Ursula as soon as possible, and he had reason to want that. They had been nothing but a nuisance to him ever since Ursula had abandoned her to go running off to Ankara!

It was completely dark when they crossed the square and went into the café opposite. Mark ordered two glasses of tea and drank his, lazily watching her as she struggled to hold the hot glass with the same panache that he did.

"Cheer up, Melâhat," he said. "Eyüp is a renowned miracle-worker, but he doesn't care to be rushed. We shall both have to learn to be patient."

She wasn't sure that she knew what he was talking about, but his voice was warm and he had called her Melâhat in the way she liked. She felt herself relax, the tension leaving her, and she felt able to laugh and joke again. Her tea had cooled, too, sufficiently for her to be able to drink it without burning her fingers and her lips. For the moment it was enough for her that she was with him and that he appeared to welcome her society.

It was raining hard when they went out again into the street. Mark gave her a meaning look and shook his head when she started back for the place where they had alighted from the bus.

"I think not," he said dryly. "You'll find a *dolmus* taxi more comfortable, no doubt, than struggling on and off another bus!"

"I don't mind going by bus," she assured him.

"Well, I do!" he retorted. "Another trip like that would give me grey hairs! We'll go by taxi and you can behave yourself!"

. "It wasn't *me* –" she protested.

"Wasn't it just!" he said grimly. "And don't look at me with those melting eyes, or I won't be responsible for seeing you home safely! You have been warned!"

Madeleine gave a little skip of pleasure. "Must we go home?"

He put up a hand and gave her cheek a playful slap. "Your reckless love of adventure again?"

She subsided into the *domus* taxi that was passing them,

135

pulling her coat from under Mark as he sat down beside her. "No," she said, "but I've enjoyed myself. It's been lovely! I like doing your notes, I don't want you to think I don't, but it isn't the same as seeing these places for myself!"

He looked at her in the darkness of the cab and she saw him smile. "I've enjoyed it too, but Ursula is staying in my house too, and I owe her some of my time as her host. We've left her on her own for long enough!"

Ursula was seated in the sitting-room when they came in. The pinched look round her mouth told its own story of the fury that burned within her.

"How dared you?" she said to Madeleine. "You knew I didn't feel well! Where have you been? Don't stand there dripping on to Mark's carpet! Go and change, and then come back here and explain yourself!"

"But you said I could go out, Mrs. Adeney!"

Ursula made a play of looking at her watch. "That was a good six hours ago! I thought you meant a short walk, or maybe to do some shopping, not to disappear for half a day!"

Madeleine bit her lip. "I'm sorry," she said.

Ursula's eyes played over her face thoughtfully before turning to Mark. "Do I have to thank you for bringing her home?" she asked him languidly. "I can't believe that you asked for her company, so I can only presume that she foisted herself on you somehow, and apologise."

Madeleine hung her head, not daring to look at Mark. She supposed, in a way, she had made it difficult for him not to escort her into the Süleymaniye, but after that, surely the choice had been his?

"Madeleine shouldn't have been out alone," Mark said evenly. "She's interested in the notes she's been typing for me and I was pleased to show her some of the more interesting buildings of Istanbul in exchange."

"Oh?" Ursula drawled. "Madeleine, go and change! I have

136

something to say to my brother-in-law and I prefer not to have you listening to every word we say!"

"I'm sorry," Madeleine said again. She hurried out of the room and up the stairs, shaking out her wet hair as she went. It didn't matter what Ursula said, it had been worth it! Every minute of it! She would remember it for ever!

It didn't take her long to change into a light dress and high-heeled shoes. There was no point in putting on anything more glamorous when she had promised to finish typing Mark's notes for him that evening. She would have preferred to lie on her bed and dream of the things he had said to her, but she could imagine his caustic comments if she did! Perhaps she did confuse romance and reality, but for her the two fused into the one in him, and they always would, as long as they both were alive.

When she came downstairs again, she could hear Ursula's raised voice in the hall. "I'll send her back to London! Mark, can't you see how I can't allow anything else to come between us? Darling, I've been so miserable since Bob was killed. I can't manage by myself!"

"Then sell out," Mark advised coolly. "There's no one to stop you!"

"Have you no feeling for Adeney Publications at all?" she demanded.

"Yes," he said. "The life of a business executive was never for me, but I would have made a better job of it than Bob did. I should have seen just where you were driving him, my dear, and done something about it. Is that clear enough for you?"

Madeleine tapped nervously at the door, unwilling to overhear any more of what had certainly not been intended for her ears.

"My word, I might have known you'd be back with your ears flapping!" Ursula exclaimed. "Come in, why don't you? I'm sure Mark would like a witness while he accuses me of the next best thing to murder!"

"Not murder," Mark said. "Ambition and greed, and a ruthless desire to get your own way. Bob was no match for you and you knew it. Was that why you chose to marry him?"

"*Yes!*"

Mark's expression broke into the travesty of a smile. "Did he know?" was all he asked.

Ursula's face was very white. The pinched look round her mouth intensified and she looked far older· than her years. "That's why he went to Viet-Nam. He said he was leaving the field clear for you –"

"Think again! He knew I wanted out, that that was all I'd wanted since long before you came on the scene! You know, Ursula, you'd be a pretty formidable person if you could only be honest with yourself. What you mean is that Bob slipped through your fingers and I was the only alternative in sight. You'd have preferred someone else, though, wouldn't you? You've never been quite sure that if I chose to tangle with you, I wouldn't be the one to emerge as victor. Well, it's an experiment I don't choose to try –"

"I only want you to work for me!" Ursula blazed back at him. "Did you think I wanted anything more? Oh no, my dear, I'm not cut out to be the complacent wife the woman you married would have to be!"

Mark raised his eyebrows and actually grinned. "But then nobody's asked you!" he observed.

Fascinated, Madeleine watched while the other girl's expression changed from outraged petulance to reluctant laughter. "You're a brute!" Ursula told Mark. "I hate you! And just for that, you can take me out somewhere decent this evening. If you can spare a whole afternoon for Madeleine's entertainment, I don't see why you shouldn't make a similar sacrifice for me!"

Mark shrugged. "No sacrifice! Where do you want to go?"

"Anywhere. A nightclub, if you know of a respectable one that I wouldn't be ashamed to be seen in?"

"Right, a nightclub it shall be." He turned his head slightly to include Madeleine in his smile. "It looks as though you'll have to change again –"

"No, she's not coming!" Ursula said flatly.

"I have your notes to finish," Madeleine reminded him. She felt *de trop* and awkward, a feeling that she was beginning to associate with Ursula.

"If you don't come, we shan't go," Mark said, the mockery plain in his eyes, as if he knew that she wouldn't care to cross him, whatever she did to Ursula.

"Don't mind me!" Ursula put in.

"Well, Madeleine?"

She nodded quickly. "But I'm quite happy to stay here and finish your notes!"

"The noble secretary!" Ursula observed. "It looks as though we're stuck with you, so you'd better go and change again, as Mark suggests. Something *quiet*, if you can manage it. I don't want you attracting a whole lot of undesirable attention to yourself."

Mark's mocking laughter did nothing for Madeleine's composure. She glared at him with a hard-won touch of haughtiness. She was hard put to it not to echo her employer's cry of hate. She might have done, too, but she had a sudden memory of how he had said *Hullo, Melâhat!* in the very same way when he had first seen her, and she could not resist her heart.

"I'll go and change," she said.

Madeleine's experience of nightclubs was strictly limited. She followed Mark and Ursula down a flight of stairs. They made a very handsome couple together, she thought, perhaps especially as Mark was standing one step behind his sister-in-law, giving him greater height. He had such a commanding presence that one was apt to overlook the fact that he was scarcely any taller than Ursula. He was taller than Madeleine, of course, but then her lack of inches had long been a joke in her family, and most people looked down on her.

He looked back at her up the stairs and she hurried down to join them, intrigued by the red glow that came from the room below. Ursula gave an impatient lift to her shoulders and marched firmly through the door, pausing, her head held high, in the entrance, while a waiter found a table for the three of them and took their order for drinks.

"It looks as if we're just in time for the first show," Ursula said with satisfaction. "I do hope that it won't be a succession of belly-dancers. They may do something for the men, but they bore me stiff!"

In this she was unlucky. The first of the dancers barely went up on to the platform at all, but posed fleetingly beside every man in the room, a glassy smile fixed to her face, while the flashlights popped and the camera recorded the moment in black and white for all time.

"I knew it!" Ursula complained. "Surely she must be able to do something else?"

Madeleine was on the point of telling her about the gypsy dancers who had entertained her and Mark when they had gone out for dinner before, but she thought better of it, and fixed her attention on the next dancer, who was as dedicated to her art as the previous girl had been dull.

It was inevitable that when she chose a man to go up on to the stage with her, she would choose Mark. It was equally inevitable that he should welcome the attention. He showed not the slightest sign of being aware of the rest of the audience, but stood, completely sure of himself, watching the girl critically. Once, he said something to her and from merely going through the motions of the dance, the girl jerked upright and began again, her whole being changed into a vivid, sensual channel of emotion, dancing only for him, her eyes fixed on his, as she went from height to height of sinuous motion in her efforts to please him.

"I wonder if there's a single daughter of Eve who'd stand

up to him and not invite him to walk all over her?" Ursula mused. Her eyes left the dance and rested on Madeleine's face. "If you think he has time for any woman, look at him now! All the giving has to be on her side, while he criticises and tells her to do better! That's Mark Adeney for you!"

"However he did it, he's inspired her to dance considerably better than she was before," Madeleine observed. She watched the girl's delighted response as Mark handed her a bank-note and kissed her lightly on the cheek, putting his hand on her bare back with undisguised pleasure.

"Another of his lady-friends!" Ursula murmured. "I wonder why he brought us here to see her. Perhaps he meant to warn us, if we need the warning, that he has no intention of cutting down on his pleasures for either of us. Unnecessary, of course, but like him, don't you think?"

Madeleine didn't answer. She averted her face as Mark came back to join them, wishing that, like Ursula, she could change her expression with a flicker of her eyelashes and congratulate him on the girl's performance. Instead, she took a sip from the glass in front of her and choked over the dryness of the Martini she had been given. In the turmoil that followed, she almost missed Ursula's sudden stiffening and the whiteness of her face. Madeleine coughed again and blew her nose on Mark's proffered handkerchief, thanking him weakly as she returned it.

"Mark, look who's over there!" The urgency in Ursula's voice brought Madeleine's eyes to where she was pointing as well. A tall man, dressed in the uniform of the United States Army, rose slowly to his feet and made his way through the crowded tables towards them.

"May I join you?" he asked. He ignored Ursula's proffered hand and spoke directly to Madeleine. "You look as though you're having more fun over here than I am on my own over there. Do you mind?"

Madeleine stared back at him. "Not at all," she said, her

141

eyes wide. Was *he* the reason for Ursula's Ankara visit? Was it possible? He was so ordinary! Especially when compared with Mark, who was not ordinary at all!

He sat down on the spindly chair that Mark found for him, with his back almost to Ursula. "It doesn't look as though we're going to be introduced," he remarked with a wry smile that made him look much younger than he was. "I'm Oliver Welland."

CHAPTER X

"*Colonel* Oliver Welland," he said, just in case she had missed his rank emblazoned on his uniform.

"Yes, I noticed," she murmured. She cast Ursula an uneasy look, but that lady was listening to something that Mark was saying to her, her shoulders raised a trifle as a barrier between herself and Madeleine. "Wh – what are you doing in Istanbul?" she asked Colonel Welland.

"I came to see someone," he answered. "I had a couple of days off from the discussions we've been having in Ankara, so I thought I'd look this person up." His eyes slid over Ursula's unresponsive figure. "I'd counted on a better reception. I should have known better!" He forced a smile. "Still, it isn't all loss, since I've met you. Are you prepared to take pity on a lonely soldier and show him the sights?"

Colonel Welland's hair was beginning to grey at the temples, but cut short in a boyish style it made him look younger than his years. His charm was as gawky and adolescent as his looks on the surface, but there was no doubt that underneath he was both competent and as hard as steel. If she were wise, Madeleine thought, she would not get involved in whatever lay between him and Ursula. Neither of them would thank her for it.

"Madeleine is always game to go sightseeing," Mark drawled mockingly.

"But not tomorrow," Madeleine said as firmly as she could. "I have work to do tomorrow."

Colonel Welland shook his head at her. "I only have tomorrow. It'd be a kindness if you'd take pity on me."

Madeleine refused to meet the appeal in his eyes. "Thank

143

you," she murmured, and then in case that had sounded ungracious: "I'd like to."

Mark uttered an explosive laugh that sent the colour racing to her cheeks. "Where will you go?" he asked them.

Colonel Welland shrugged his shoulders. "I guess I'd like to see the covered bazaar. I'm told that it isn't what it was, but then what is? Besides, I'd like to find a souvenir or two while I'm here. Apart from that, I'll leave it to the lady to decide. I'm easy!"

"You flatter yourself!" Ursula assured him dryly. "However, it's your fault if you're bored stiff!"

"You think so?" he grunted. "Come again, Ursula my love! I think you have some responsibility in the matter."

Madeleine was thankful when the floor show resumed, claiming their attention. A group of dancers took the floor, all of them playing little brass cymbals between their forefingers and thumbs and shaking their bodies rather like so many wet dogs emerging from a swim. They were followed by another belly-dancer who came and went almost immediately, to be replaced by the Spanish star of the show, a flamenco singer who was greatly appreciated by the local audience.

When the last strains died away, Ursula began to gather her wraps together making it clear that she was ready to go. Mark followed her lead, helping her on with her coat. Madeleine put on her own coat, only too aware that Colonel Welland was using her as a substitute for his real interest.

"Shall I pick you up at your place tomorrow?" he asked her as she hurried for the door.

"If it isn't too far out of your way," she answered.

"I guess I'll manage. How do I get across to the Asian side?"

She told him, her eyes on Ursula's retreating figure going fast up the stairs. "I'll have to go! They may not wait for me!"

Colonel Welland looked surprised. "Why shouldn't they?"

She held her handbag very tightly to her. "I don't think she's very pleased that you asked me —"

"Ursula? She's a hard case, my dear. She doesn't give a rap what I do!"

"But I work for her!" Madeleine burst out.

"Tough luck! You shouldn't give her the pleasure of seeing that she gets to you, though. Ursula thrives on power over other people. It's not her most endearing trait."

"I must go!" Madeleine said again. She thought that Mark might have waited for her, but he hadn't even noticed that she had dropped behind. It was that which hurt far more than anything Ursual could do to her. "Goodbye, Colonel Welland."

"You'd better make it Oliver," he said.

"Oh, thank you." She hesitated. "My name is Madeleine."

He smiled, evidently amused. "Yes, I know." He followed her up the stairs, putting a friendly hand on her shoulder. "We'll make tomorrow a day to remember, shall we?"

Madeleine only nodded. She ran up the last few steps and practically collided with Mark at the top. "I thought you'd gone on," she informed him breathlessly. "I didn't want to be left behind!"

"I won't lose you that easily," he said.

She felt oddly comforted. "I wish you were coming to the bazaar too tomorrow," she hazarded, half-hoping to cozen him into going with them.

"Oliver should give you a good time," he responded.

"But —" She became aware of Ursula's impatient glance in her direction and broke off what she had been going to say. Mark's eyes appraised her thoughtfully.

"Besides," he said, "I've other fish to fry tomorrow."

He would have, of course, she thought, but how she wished it was otherwise and that he had nothing better to do but to be with her!

The leash Ursula had been keeping on her temper snapped

suddenly. "This time you've gone too far!" she turned on Madeleine. "I've reminded you before that you're not here to enjoy yourself, but to serve me! The least you could have done was to ask if I had any objection to your gallivanting about Istanbul with one of my friends!"

"But if you objected, why didn't you say so?" Madeleine retorted. "I wish you had!"

"It looked like it! Oliver is a very attractive man –"

"Then why don't you go with him?" Madeleine said furiously.

"That's none of your business! I can't think what's got into you, Mad. We got along all right before! Why do you have to do everything you can to annoy me now? I didn't bring you here to amuse yourself with my friends, but to make things easier for *me*! If you're not careful, my dear, I'll send a report on you back to London that will cost you your job. So, before you go falling for Oliver, you'd better think again!"

"That's enough!" Mark said easily. "Save it, Ursula, until you're home and don't have a crowd of people watching, if you don't mind. Madeleine had no choice but to accept Oliver's invitation and you know it!"

"I know that you won't hear a word against *my* employee, but that doesn't change my opinion of her –"

"Nor mine of you!" Madeleine exploded, exasperated.

"*Mad!*"

"And don't call me that! I don't like it!"

To the surprise of the two girls, Mark burst into laughter. "*That* figures!" He took both of them by the arm, walking determinedly between them. "Come on, my pretty ones, let's go home!"

They went home in silence. Even Ursula submitted to Mark's force of will, Madeleine noticed. She knew that he had heard enough of them quarrelling, and the funny thing was that she didn't seem to resent it as she would have done from anyone else. But then Ursula didn't mind postponing her rebukes. She could keep her anger on ice much longer than any-one else Madeleine had ever known, whereas her own anger geysered up in an instant and was gone as quickly. Probably, when they got back to Mark's house, Ursula would start all over again – She sighed audibly, aware of how tired she was and how disappointing the end had been of an almost perfect day.

When they went into the house, however, Mark sent her straight up to bed. "Don't take all the hot water!" he adjured her. He ran a finger across the top of her head and smiled into her eyes. "Sleep well," he said. "Pleasant dreams of Eyüp, and may your request come true!"

She shook her head slowly, knowing that it never would. "Good night," she said quickly, and hurried away from him up the stairs.

Oliver Welland took no pleasure in the *yali*. "What does any-one want to live over here for?" he demanded. "Why can't he live in the Beyoglu district like everyone else?"

Madeleine tried to resist the quick, defensive retort that rose to her lips. "It's very easy, really," she said instead. "There's a ferry service that comes and goes from just beside the Dolmabahçe Palace."

Oliver winced. "And how do we get from there to the cov-ered bazaar? This place is impossible when it comes to getting about. If I'd known, I'd have met you somewhere more cen-tral!"

"I'm sorry," Madeleine said. "But we can take the ferry back to the Galata Bridge. It isn't far to walk from there."

"I guess we'll have to!"

Madeleine's spirits drooped. He had barely looked at her since she had let him in and she guessed that he was hoping to catch sight of Ursula. He probably thought that it still wasn't too late to change partners and to take Ursula shopping with him instead of "the little secretary", as he probably thought of

147

here. But Ursula was still in her bed and had shown no signs of wanting to see any more of Oliver Welland for a long time to come. She had summoned Madeleine into her presence that morning and had sourly told her to make the most of her date and have a good time. She had added that it had been ridiculous of Madeleine to have said she'd go in the first place. Oliver Welland might look a young man, but he was quite old enough to be her father!

"Yes, I know," Madeleine had said surprisingly.

"Then why –"

"I felt sorry for him," Madeleine had confessed.

Ursula had laughed brutally at that. "Oliver's the last person to need your pity, my dear. You look out for yourself!"

"I will," Madeleine had promised.

Oliver was now walking along beside her, his eyes on the ground, almost as if he were afraid that if he looked across the Bosphorus to the magnificent skyline of Old Stamboul he might find something to enjoy in his surroundings. Out of uniform, he looked as though his clothes didn't belong to him but had been borrowed from a younger, flashier brother.

"I'm told it's easy to get lost in the covered bazaar," Madeleine said, making conversation. "It's the largest in the world. What sort of thing do you want to buy?"

Oliver didn't know. "Something gold for Ursula," he said eventually. "Only the very best is good enough for Ursula, and there's nothing better than gold!"

Madeleine breathed out slowly. "Will she want to accept a valuable present from you just now?" she asked as gently as she could. "I mean, I'm sure she's very fond of you, but gold is costly –"

"Ursula's never turned down a present yet!" he cut in wryly. "I guess you don't know her very well, Madeleine. How long have you been travelling with her? She didn't bring you to Ankara, did she?"

"No."

148

The cold monosyllable had no visible effect on him. "I thought not. I thought she had come to Turkey on her own because she'd heard that I was here. When she came to Ankara I was sure of it! But I guess Adeney Publications still owns her body and soul, and I come nowhere in her scheme of things."

"Have you known her long?" Madeleine asked, guiding him firmly on to the ferry. She was busy with her own thoughts. Mark would never have expected her to buy the tickets and to struggle with the Turkish directions of how they were to find the covered market when they left the ferry.

"I knew her when she still wore socks," Oliver told her. "I knew them all for a time. I even went to the wedding, though heaven knows I didn't want to! That was destined to failure right from the start!" He was silent for a long moment, staring gloomily down into the waters of the Bosphorus. "Bob didn't know how to handle her. If he'd lived, I'd have had something to say to him when he got back from Viet-Nam! A married man hasn't the right to go risking his life on the other side of the world if he doesn't have to. What did he expect? That Ursula would thank him for going?"

"I thought he wanted to go," Madeleine put in.

"Honey, he couldn't get away fast enough! She ran him ragged whenever they were together. He was a quiet, contented chap with a job that he liked and which didn't demand too much from him. But that didn't suit her! She married him for Adeney Publications' potential, knowing exactly where she was going. Bob didn't know what had hit him! He stood the pace for as long as he could and then he got out from under the only way he knew how. It was no surprise that he got himself killed – no surprise to me anyway. I would have married Ursula then and there, but I wasn't having Adeney Publications hanging like some albatross around our marriage. I told her she had to choose. Who needs you? she said. Nor did she! The whole of Washington sits up and takes notice when she runs one of her campaigns in her magazine, and she sits in the sun and eats it all up, sure of herself and where she's going. Only it isn't what she really wants at all!"

"No?" Madeleine queried. It wasn't quite how she saw Ursula Adeney, but she was fascinated to know what he thought the American girl really wanted.

"No! Ursula is a small town girl, with small town ambitions at heart! What she wants is a husband who can make his own pile without any help from her, and a home with nice neighbours, and some children to worry over and love. That's what she'd get if she married me!"

Oh dear, Madeleine thought. As a future, it might suit herself, whose ambitions had never been anything out of the ordinary, but *Ursula*? He must be round the bend if he thought that Ursula would transplant to a desirable residence in a pleasant suburb such as he envisaged. She would stifle in a fortnight – less, in a day! She hadn't built up an enterprise like Adeney Publications on a simple, girl-next-door desire for a cosy nest in some obscure part of America. She was born to be in the centre of great affairs, bending the world to her will. Couldn't he see that?

"You don't believe me," Oliver said, stating the obvious with a gallant but superior smile. "Ursula doesn't either just now, but then she never did understand herself very well. If she'd really wanted anything different, she'd have married Mark and not his brother. If Bob had kept his head and said no to her every now and again, they might have stood a chance together. But it wasn't in Bob to say no to anyone, and now she's got the bit well and truly between her teeth. But you can't tell me that she's happy! She's scared stiff of the high position she's climbed to. Did you know that she suffers from vertigo? That's why she loathes sight-seeing. No, truly, she hates not having her feet on the ground! But she needn't think that I'm going to rescue her from her lonely hilltop. She can climb down herself and lose a little of that dignity she thinks is so precious to her! She'll find it warmer down in the valley with me and I'll welcome her with open arms, but I'm not forcing her into it, much as she'd like me to. If I gave her a handle like that, I'd never hear the end of it whenever she felt like it and things weren't going too well. No, sir! I'm no Bob Adeney, to be talked into an early grave. If anyone has any recriminations to make, it's going to be me!" He grinned. "You don't give much for my chances, do you?"

"Frankly, no," Madeleine admitted.

"You may be right. But I still hope she'll come round this time. She will if Mark stands firm."

Madeleine went cold. "Do you think he might not?"

Oliver looked up as the ferry edged into its berth beside the Galata Bridge. "We've arrived!" he announced unnecessarily. "Where do we go from here?"

"It isn't far," Madeleine assured him. She pulled a map out of her pocket and consulted it, trying to remember the instructions she had received at the ticket office. "We go up there," she said, pointing.

Oliver stared up the steep slope ahead of them. "Oh well," he said, "let's get ashore, shall we?"

The crowds streamed off the ferry in the extraordinary silence with which the Turks do everything except drive. Madeleine dived through the dark-clad mass, wanting to get away from Oliver and yet not wanting to. Oliver knew exactly what lay between Mark and Ursula. He probably knew whether Mark wanted to go back to the States with Ursula, and that was something Madeleine wanted to know too. She had to know! She had to have time to get used to the idea that she wouldn't see him again. Somehow she had to live with this dead weight of despair that gripped her whenever she thought of life without Mark. She had to prepare herself for that.

"I think you're in better training than I am," Oliver objected as they crossed the road. "Slow down! I'll be dead on arrival if we keep up this pace!"

Madeleine slowed her steps to suit him. It was another reminder of how different today was from yesterday. Yesterday it had been she who had dawdled behind. She had been in no hurry then!

"Did Mark want to marry Ursula too?" she asked abruptly.

Oliver looked surprised. "What makes you ask that?" he countered.

"I shouldn't, I suppose," Madeleine admitted. "But I have to know! Ursula seems to think that Mark is in love with her — and I think she's right!"

Oliver stopped walking altogether, allowing his eyes to wander slowly over the minarets and domes of the mosques ahead of him in silence. "There was a time," he said at last, "when I thought Mark would have liked to have cut his brother out, but if he was in love with Ursula he managed to comfort himself for his loss very quickly. Mark has never been short of girl-friends." His eyes slid over Madeleine's scarlet cheeks and he raised his eyebrows in mute enquiry. "Have you a personal interest in all this?"

"Not really," Madeleine said.

Oliver regarded her thoughtfully. "Mark isn't at all like his brother," he went on. "I doubt he'd sell his soul for Adeney Publications, even with Ursula as bait."

"A very luscious bait," Madeleine said.

"That," said Oliver, "is all in the eye of the beholder, my dear. I grant that she dazzles me, but Mark —? Mark doesn't only want to come first, he has to be master —

"He isn't egotistical!" Madeleine protested sharply. "He's very kind and — and why shouldn't he take what he wants? He doesn't *hurt* anybody!"

"I didn't say he was an egoist," Oliver said. "Though he has every reason to be when even his victims leap to his defence! I think I envy him rather — most men do! But that doesn't mean that I want Ursula to have anything to do with him. He'd demolish her where it really hurts, in her good opinion of herself and her attraction for the opposite sex!''

Madeleine only shook her head. She knew better! Mark's hands were firm, but they were very gentle. He, too, liked the heights, but not the giddy heights of power. His were the heights of love, demanding a self-giving that Ursula knew nothing about, and which Madeleine herself had only glimpsed. But to be loved by Mark would be the ultimate sharing, sharing one's body, mind and spirit without even those reserves of privacy that one feared to expose to another. Mark would demand all, but he would give unreservedly in return. It was hard to know that she would probably never be loved by Mark, but she would never regret knowing him. He had taught her what being a woman could mean – and he had kissed her, once or twice.

Oliver said: "How far away is this place? I believe we're lost!"

"No, we're not!" Madeleine looked about her and gave a quick exclamation of delight as she recognized some of the tatty stalls that surrounded the entrance of the covered bazaar, selling plastic buckets and hideous, highly coloured cloth pictures that are loved everywhere in the Middle East. "We're here!"

She led the way into the bazaar, a little startled herself by the sight that met her eyes. The alleyways were more or less in straight lines, dark except for the electric light bulbs that burned continuously in the tiny shops that spilt out of the small cupboards where they were supposed to carry on their business. Those selling the same wares were grouped together, the goldsmiths, the shoeshops, even the furniture shops where men staggered up and down the narrow alley with enormous wardrobes, beds and armchairs strapped to their sturdy backs. Oliver, however, was only interested in the goldsmiths. To Madeleine's undiscerning eye they all looked exactly the same, but Oliver knew better. He went from one to another, in an endless labour of love, determined to find the best buy of all to give to Ursula. Madeleine felt superfluous and, quite soon, she felt bored as well. Large lumps of gold held little appeal for her, and though she found the thousands of gold bangles, the lockets, the charms to keep the evil eye away, and all the other golden pieces quite pretty, she didn't particularly want any of them for herself.

"Ursula wears a lot of bracelets," Oliver mused, "but I've never seen her wear a ring. Odd, but I've never even seen her wear a wedding ring."

Madeleine suppressed a yawn. Come to think of it, she had never seen any rings on Ursula's hands either, but then Ursula had ugly masculine-looking hands that she wouldn't want to draw attention to. And that was odd. Madeleine would have supposed that Ursula had enough confidence for anything but it seemed that that was not so.

"Shall I buy her a ring?"

"Yes, why not?" Madeleine said. Anything to get away from these claustrophobic passages of glittering shops. "Or one of those bracelets," she suggested. It was hardly kind to take her a ring if she didn't like them.

"I'll buy her a ring!"

The purchase took as long as the search. The owner of the shop served them tea, bidding them sit down on two rickety chairs that he produced from the depths of his establishment. The tea was pale and drunk from tulip-shaped glasses while the ring was neatly packaged up and handed over to Oliver with a flourish. "I trust you find yourself welcome in Istanbul," the shopkeeper exclaimed happily. "There is much to see! Very beautiful city! Very lovely people!"

Madeleine agreed with him with an almost indecent haste. "We want to see the Blue Mosque today," she told him, hoping that he wouldn't think it forward of her to be keeping up the customer's end of the conversation. "I've always wanted to see it! Haven't you, Oliver?"

"Never heard of it!"

"Oh, really! Of course you have!" Madeleine dismissed him with a frown, turning back to the shopkeeper. "How do we get to it from here?" she asked.

He explained to her carefully exactly which way she should go, adding that she should be sure and look for the original tiles that still remained on the lower parts of the walls and in the galleries, for where the old had been replaced by modern copies, the designs were often feeble and the colours crude.

"Do we really have to go there?" Oliver groaned.

Madeleine hesitated. "I'd like to – if you don't mind. I've never seen it, you see. I wanted to see Sinan's mosques first –"

"You've lost me! But if you want to go, we'll go!"

He was as good as his word, but his face fell when he was expected to take off his shoes, and his discomfort turned into active dislike as they stepped into the magnificent prayer-hall. He didn't like the feeling of space, nor the soaring dome, nor the fantastic tiles of floral designs displaying the lily, rose, carnation and, of course, the tulip. "It's a bit much," was all he said.

Madeleine, however, had forgotten all about him. She was lost in a whirl of subtle blues and greens, beautifully lit by the two hundred and sixty windows. The white Proconesian marble of the *mihrab* and *mimber* caught at her emotions, so fine was the carving. And then there were the great courtyard doors and the woodwork that was encrusted with ivory and mother-of-pearl. Last of all, she saw the ceiling of the Sultan's lodge, away up in an upper gallery on the left. It was wooden and painted in the most gorgeous colours in arabesques of floral and geometrical designs in a style she had never seen before. It was, without doubt, one of the most beautiful buildings she had ever seen or hoped to see.

"Let's go!" Oliver's voice broke into her consciousness, recalling her to reality. "I want to give Ursula her ring!"

Madeleine nodded, beyond speech. Somehow, by hook or by crook, she would come back, she decided. She would come back and she would see it all again.

Madeleine was glad to be rid of Oliver. She set up the typewriter on the table and arranged the last of Mark's notes in a neat pile beside her. His writing hadn't become any more readable since she had last seen it and she had to give it all her attention, puzzling over the bits that she couldn't make out. And so it was that she didn't hear Mark come into the room and he leaned over the back of her chair and blew gently on the top of her head. She was very conscious of him then and her breath caught in her throat, making it impossible for her to say anything.

He picked up a lock of her hair between two fingers and pulled at it gently. "What did you do with Oliver?" he asked.

"He's with Ursula." Her voice sounded high and strained and she swallowed convulsively.

"Did you enjoy your outing?" Mark went on conversationally. The mockery in his voice was very apparent, as if he already knew the answer.

"Oliver bought Ursula a ring," she said in a rush. "We went to the Blue Mosque! It was beautiful! Only Oliver didn't like it!"

"No, he wouldn't," Mark said. "You should have kept it for later, when I can take you myself –"

"W – will you?"

"Probably. I shall like to see you against a background of fabulous tiles. You'd suit each other." He pulled on the lock of hair still held in his fingers. "So Oliver didn't appeal to you!"

"I didn't say that!"

He grinned suddenly at her distress. "You didn't have to! What are you doing with those notes, by the way? They won't be any more legible when you've finished crushing them up like that!"

"No," she said. She pulled herself away from him, making a great play of reading the piece of paper in front of her. Mark laughed softly and stood up straight, turning away from her to go out of the room. But she couldn't bear for him to go! She turned in her chair, gripping the paper as if her life depended on it.

"Maruk Bey!"

He turned immediately, his eyes very bright. "Yes?" he said.

Her face flamed and she could have bitten out her tongue. Slowly the blush grew redder still, until there was no part of her that couldn't feel the burning heat of her embarrassment. Mark's expression did nothing to comfort her, but he said nothing. He took the paper out of her hand and read it through for her, laying it back on the table beside her. The mockery in his expression made the backs of her hands tingle. She could not have moved if the house had gone on fire.

When she finally made herself turn round to face him, she found he had gone, and she didn't know whether to be glad or sorry. Only one thing was certain: she had not heard a single word of the note he had read out to her.

CHAPTER XI

THE notes were finished, and leaving a void in Madeleine's life. She now had nothing to do, for Ursula resented her going out by herself, although she herself was almost constantly in Oliver's presence. She had accepted Oliver's ring, Madeleine noticed, though it seemed to have little meaning for her. Perhaps Americans exchanged rings more readily and without significance? Madeleine had no means of telling, but she thought not. It was probably just another of the idiosyncrasies of her employer.

Of Mark she saw just as little, but she wouldn't dwell on that. Instead, she read his books, eagerly learning all she could about his chosen subject and even more about the buildings and peoples of the eastern end of the Mediterranean. She was careful only to take one volume at a time to her room because she had had no opportunity to ask him if she might borrow from his shelves. She didn't think he would mind, but she had no intention of drawing Ursula's attention to what she was doing, for she minded almost anything these days.

It was the middle of the morning when Madeleine came downstairs after helping Mihrimar with the beds. She had finished a book on the everyday life in Ottoman Turkey and thought she had seen a companion volume on life in Byzantine times which she planned to take back to her room with her, to entertain her through the long hours of the afternoon. But when she reached the outside of the door, she could hear Ursula's voice, raised in anger, inside the sitting room and paused for a minute, wondering whether she should go away again. The words came clearly to her and she froze as she began to make sense of them. If she had wanted to move after that, she could not have brought herself to do it.

"Mark darling, this is like old times after all, isn't it?"

"It has a familiar ring to it!" Mark's voice came wryly and quite clearly through the door. "But it isn't quite the same."

"Still jealous?"

"I never was jealous of Bob —"

"Mark! How can you say so? You spent hours trying to talk him out of marrying me! He told me so! And you have to admit that you were quite smitten with me yourself!"

"I don't deny it," Mark agreed without hesitation. "But marriage wasn't exactly what I had in mind, and Bob had. If you had been another woman I would have rejoiced with him, but you already had your eyes on Washington, hadn't you? Bob was no more than a stepping-stone to take you there."

"A very willing stepping-stone!"

"I daresay there were compensations — at first. Where are you going from here, Ursula?"

There was a short silence and Madeleine strained her ears to hear what was going on, then Ursula drawled, her voice husky, and yes, excited: "That depends on you, darling!"

"Back to the States?"

"Of course, if you come with me. You will, won't you? I'm offering you — *everything*, Mark! I won't interfere in your management of Adeney Publications, I promise you. I'll be too busy bringing up the heir to the enterprise. You'd like that, wouldn't you?"

"Aren't you getting a bit ahead of yourself?" Mark asked.

"But you've always wanted to marry me!" Ursula protested.

Madeleine could imagine the mockery on Mark's face. "My dear, if you can persuade yourself of that, you can persuade yourself of anything!"

"But you wanted me —"

"That isn't quite the same thing!"

Madeleine swallowed. Poor Ursula! But she must have known! Why, even Madeleine, the born unsophisticate, knew that Mark had wanted her too, but she had known quite well that he wouldn't marry her. Why should he? He relished his freedom, and what had she to offer him in place of that?

"I'm offering you your inheritance," Ursula said. "I'm offering you Adeney Publications, Mark! Doesn't that mean anything to you?"

"I'm afraid not. Power politics has never been my scene. When it was a small venture, involved in local affairs and doing it well, I had quite an affection for the business, but now I wouldn't give you that for it!" He clicked his fingers sharply together. "I'm sorry, Ursula, you'll have to think again. I've accepted a post at the Bosphorus University for the next three years, as a matter of fact –"

"When?" The single word was spat out, holding a venom that made Madeleine wince.

"Yesterday," Mark said. He was smiling and very sure of himself. One could tell by the lilt in his voice.

"I don't believe it!" Real anguish sounded in Ursula's words. There was no doubt that she was very upset indeed.

"Oh, come now, it doesn't mean very much to you in the long run. You've managed Adeney Publications very successfully so far. Why have you cold feet about it now?"

Ursula sounded truly wretched. "It isn't as much fun as I thought it'd be! I don't like being a career woman, without a husband. I've always needed to have a man around. If you don't want Adeney Publications, I'll sell it and marry Oliver! *He* wants to marry me."

"It sounds like a good idea to me!"

"Don't you feel anything for me?" Ursula sobbed.

"A certain responsibility," Mark admitted. "I don't like to see you unhappy and lost. I think Oliver may do very well, especially if he won't dabble in the publishing business but stays on in the Army."

160

"I love Oliver!"

"Yes, I think you do," Mark agreed slowly. "As much as you love anyone apart from yourself. No offence intended, Ursula my love, but you didn't love Bob, and you certainly don't love me."

"I mean it!" Ursula burst out. "I shall sell Adeney Publications lock, stock, and barrel!"

"Do that!" Mark said gently. "Get it off all our backs. And marry your Oliver as fast as you can, my dear. Bob would be as pleased for you as I am."

"That I doubt," Ursula answered, but without resentment. "Oh dear, how *dull* life is going to be! Oliver is terribly respectable. We'll live in a comfortable home somewhere and have nice, respectable children, a pigeon pair, if Oliver can manage it, and I shall be bored silly in no time!"

Mark laughed. "You can hardly wait!"

"No, I can't," Ursula admitted. "In fact, I'll go and tell him now! I'll go back to Ankara with him and to hell with Adeney Publications! They can get themselves a new boss and welcome. Why should I worry?"

"Why indeed?" Mark agreed smoothly. "But there is one thing, before you go sailing off into Oliver's arms. What about Madeleine?"

"What about her?" Ursula retorted sharply.

"You brought her to Turkey, my dear."

"Only because the London office insisted! I didn't want her then and I don't want her now. Send her back to England, if you want to be rid of her. They can pick up the check at their end!"

"If you didn't have any use for her, why did you consent to her coming?" Mark insisted.

"Oh well, you know how it is," Ursula answered, without interest. "I didn't want them to know that I'd come to Turkey because Oliver was here. You too, of course! Only they knew you were in Istanbul and they understood that I wanted to see my own brother-in-law. But Oliver I wanted to keep to myself."

"Nevertheless," Mark told her, "you'll do something about Madeleine. She's had no money since she's been here, and you owe her something for the fright you gave her the last time you went to Ankara."

Ursula's footsteps came towards the door. "*You* do something, darling! I'm sure she'd prefer it coming from you anyway. Tell her I'm grateful for her services and pack her on the first flight back to London. I'll try to remember to send the London Office a note to give her a bonus and her back pay, but I'm not doing anything more!"

Madeleine didn't wait for Mark's comment. She felt cold all through and knew it was her own fault for eavesdropping on somebody else's conversation. It was the sort of thing that lowered one in one's own opinion of oneself for days! In fact she would have been feeling quite sick with guilt, only she was cold with anger as well. How could Ursula think of marrying Mark when she loved another man? How could she offer him counterfeit goods in such a blatant way? To Mark of all people! Madeleine could forgive her quite easily for her lack of interest in herself, but how could she attempt to do such a thing to Mark? That she could neither forget nor forgive, and she didn't think she ever would. It was shoddy, and there was absolutely nothing shoddy about Mark – even if she was being impossibly romantic to think so, as he would be the first to tell her. That was the way she felt!

Oliver arrived in time for lunch. Madeleine heard him come, but she made no attempt to go downstairs. She did go to the door of her bedroom and she heard Mark's words of greeting, followed by a silence as he was taken into the sitting room. Madeleine waited for a long time for lunch to be announced, but the minutes slid by and there was no sign of anyone eating anything.

Then, when she was least expecting it, there was the sound

of laughter from within the sitting room and they all came out into the hall.

"I'd like to get going," Oliver said loudly. "I don't want Ursula to have any opportunity to change her mind!"

"I won't do that!" said Ursula. "But I'm too excited to eat. Let's not wait for lunch."

Madeleine went down the stairs with dragging feet. She was still upset by the conversation she had overheard, the more so because she knew that she shouldn't have tarried listening in the first place. She need not have worried. Nobody noticed her at all. There was a slight skirmish as Oliver faced up to the fact that he would have to cross the Bosphorus yet again, even if it was for the last time.

"I can't understand why you choose to live on the Asian side," he said to Mark. "I'd find it a penance if I had to go by boat every time I wanted to go anywhere!"

"I like it," Mark answered. "In a way I shall be sorry when the bridge is finished and it becomes more fashionable to live on this side. Besides, I have the boat downstairs. I can always use that."

A calculating gleam crept into Ursula's eyes. "So you have," she remarked. "Mark, be a love and take us across. It would be such fun to have lunch together before we go, and you could see us off."

"Okay," Mark agreed. His eyes met Madeleine's, but it was impossible to tell what he was thinking. "We'll leave it to Madeleine to break the news to Mihrimar that nobody is going to eat her lunch."

"I'll be here," Madeleine reminded him.

He smiled straight at her. "So you will. It will be something for me to come back to!"

Her tongue felt too big for her mouth and she knew she was blushing again. "Will you find out about flights for London while you're at the airport?" she asked him.

"Do you want me to?"

She shook her head. "I can't stay here. I have to go back to England!"

He put out a hand and touched her cheek thoughtfully. "Come and see us off," he commanded. "It will give you time to think what you're going to say to Mihrimar."

She smiled. "I don't actually *say* anything to her at all, but we seem to understand one another. I don't think she'll mind everyone going."

"No?" His eyebrows shot up in a look of pure mockery. "Then I needn't have a conscience about leaving the two of you to celebrate?"

Madeleine didn't deign to answer. She was surprised to see that Ursula's bags were already packed and waiting in the hall. Oliver picked up the two heaviest, but Mark still had his hands in his pockets as he led the way down to the boathouse. Ursula followed him, laughing at some joke Oliver had cracked, as empty-handed as her brother-in-law. Madeleine sighed and picked up the remaining suitcase. It wasn't as heavy as she had expected and, gripping it lightly, she danced down the stairs behind the others, suddenly very glad that Ursula was going. Yes, she would celebrate! She would eat Mihrimar's lunch with zest and wait for Mark to come back to her. It might be the only time he ever would, but just for this one day she would pretend to herself that it was the normal thing, the way it was always going to be, all her life long.

Oliver took the suitcase from her without looking at her. She stood awkwardly on the jetty, waiting for someone to say goodbye to her. No one did. Ursula sat in the cockpit, staring out across the Bosphorus in the direction that they were going. Oliver, having stowed the luggage to his own satisfaction, joined her just as Mark let the engine rip and slid smoothly into gear. With a great thrust of power, the boat cleared the boathouse and was away, darting across the rolling waters to Europe. Madeleine lifted her hand to wave to them, but neither Oliver nor Ursula looked up. Only Mark returned her salute, and she thought, but she couldn't be sure, that he smiled at her.

Mihrimar was waiting for her in the kitchen. She held her blue beads in her hand, a well-satisfied look on her face. A flood of Turkish came out of her mouth, mixed with delighted laughter. Madeleine was more certain than ever that the blue beads were to keep the Evil Eye at bay and found herself giggling with delight as well. She checked herself with an effort, but the excitement of Ursula's departure had gone to her head like wine.

"Ogle yemegi yemek istiyorum!" she parroted in Turkish, hoping that she was saying that she would like her lunch as she thought she was.

Mihrimar nodded her head, breaking into laughter all over again. But she was pleased that Madeleine had begun to learn a few words of her language. She patted Madeleine on the shoulder, her dark eyes gleaming with that warm affection that comes so easily in the bright light of the Mediterranean.

"Maruk Bey?" she asked.

Madeleine replied with a pantomime that told her that Mark had taken the others in his boat and that he would be back later. Mihrimar gave her a teasing look and clapped her hands. There was no mistaking her meaning, and Madeleine blushed.

"Oh, but I shall be going back to England!" she declared. She said it several times, steeling herself to the knowledge that she was going home by the constant repetition of fact. "I have to go!"

"Hayir!" Mihrimar retorted. *"No!"* She shook her head. "Maruk Bey —"

But Madeleine was scarcely listening. How was she going to live without Mark when even the thought of being without him touched her with despair?

It was lonely having lunch by herself in the dining room. She half-thought that she might go out herself, but Mark had given her no time when she was to expect him home and she didn't want to miss him. He expected her to be there when he got back. He had said so.

Mihrimar brought her lunch to her, shooting the pieces of lamb off the skewer with an experienced twist of the wrist. Madeleine would have liked to have had her company, but she thought it would embarrass the Turkish woman to be asked to sit at the long polished table. There was nothing for it but to eat by herself.

Actually she enjoyed the shish-kebab, and the yoghourt that followed it. If she ate slowly enough, she thought, Mark might be back before she had finished. But one hour passed, and then another, and there was still no sign of him. Mihrimah came and cleared the table, demanding Madeleine's help with the washing up and with stripping Ursula's bed and putting the bedclothes away in the cupboard in the bathroom. Then Mihrimar, too, went back to her own house, leaving Madeleine completely alone in the *yali*, with only the oncoming shadows of evening for company.

It was quite dark when the door opened and Mark came in. Madeleine had been reading on the sofa and, although she had not known it, she had half fallen asleep in the dim light from the single lamp over her head. She jerked forward on to her feet when she heard Mark's step, holding her book in both hands behind her back.

"Did you find out about flights to London?" she demanded. "Is there one soon?"

Mark flung himself into a chair, his light-grey eyes watching her every movement. "Why are you so anxious to go back to England?"

"It's obvious!" she declared.

"To you, maybe. It isn't obvious to me."

Madeleine gave him an impatient look. "D—did Ursula and Oliver get off all right?"

He glanced at his watch. "I put them on the lunch-time

plane. Heaven help him, but the poor guy looked as though I was doing him a favour –"

"He's been in love with Ursula for ages," Madeleine interrupted. "He thinks she's basically a small town girl –"

Mark burst into laughter. "He just could be right!"

Madeleine hesitated, edging up to a confession that she had heard him talking to Ursula that morning, but in the end she couldn't find the courage to admit what she had heard. Instead, she hung her head and thought that she didn't deserve any better than to be sent packing back to London.

Mark stood up and sat down again on the sofa, picking up her book to see what she had been reading. The sardonic look he gave her when he discovered its title sent her scuttling over to the other side of the room. "This is going to be a lot of use to you in London!" he drawled.

"You don't understand!"

"No?"

"No," she said flatly. "I may come back some time. I may go to Izmir, or Ephesus, or –" She couldn't think of anywhere else in Turkey that she might visit. "I may even come back to Istanbul!" she ended with spirit.

"And you need a history of the Ottoman Empire for that?"

She stared at him. She had forgotten for the moment that that was what she had been reading. She was sure that she had had a Turkish manual as well earlier in the afternoon. What on earth could have happened to that? She hoped that it slid down the back of the sofa well out of sight and promised herself that she would rescue it later when there was no chance of his finding it.

"I like to know about the places I visit," she said.

"What did you think of the Blue Mosque?"

She was effectually silenced. It was a cruel stroke, revealing the uncomfortable truth that she had not enjoyed the visit much. Of course it was because Oliver had been bored by it, that he'd even disliked it, but if she were honest she had to admit that it was the company far more than the object of the visit that she had enjoyed at St. Sophia or at Eyüp.

"Mark, I must go back to London," she said. "And I want to go to a hotel now –"

"Isn't it rather late for that?"

She shook her head, hoping that she wasn't going to cry. "We should have gone to a hotel before! You didn't want us in your house, and I don't blame you! It wasn't fair of us to descend on you when you wanted to entertain – other people. You should have told Ursula that we were in the way!"

Mark gave her his whole attention. "What people?" he asked curiously.

She licked her lips. "*People*," she said.

His mocking smile was no help to her at all. He put out a hand and grasped her wrist, pulling her down on to the sofa beside him. "I think I shall start by entertaining you," he murmured against her ear.

"Oh no!" She twisted away from him and sat primly at the other end of the sofa, threading her fingers together in her lap. "I'm going to a hotel!"

"Oh? How do you propose to pay for your room?"

She cast him a resigned look. "But you don't want me here! Not that I mind what you do! You didn't have to stay out so long on my account! I could have gone to my room – or visited Mihrimar, or *anything*!"

"Melâhat." His voice was so gentle that she turned and looked at him despite herself. "Don't be silly!"

"I'm not!" she pleaded. "Only –"

"Only you have an impossibly romantic view of life! Now what are you looking so guilty about? You look more like a Madeleine when you're wondering if you should confess all. What happened? Did Oliver kiss you?"

Her cheeks burned. "Of course not!" she denied.

"Good," he said easily.

"He couldn't talk about anything else but Ursula!" Madeleine added. "Besides, I don't go round kissing people!"

"Oh, Melâhat darling! You kissed me!"

There was no denying that, so she maintained a dignified silence while she searched her mind for some devastating comment that would rob him of his natural advantage. But all she could think of was that he had called her *darling*, and he had sounded as though he meant it, and how very much she wished he would call her that again.

"Well?" he prompted her.

"I heard you talking to Ursula this morning," she said in a rush. "I – I listened! D-did you love her before she married your brother?"

He didn't look in the least bit shocked. On the contrary, the bright gleam of amusement in his light grey eyes told her that he quite expected her to indulge in eavesdropping, which was not particularly flattering whichever way she looked at it.

"I thought I did – for a while. I was a bit of a romantic myself at that age and I rather fancied myself as the thwarted lover –"

Madeleine giggled. "I don't believe it!"

"I assure you," he went on solemnly, "I was very earnest about it!"

"But never *thwarted*!"

"Well, no," he admitted modestly, "not often. And I became rather less earnest, which made it all much more enjoyable, but it had very little to do with love. My dear girl, do you really imagine that I ever had anything in common with Ursula?"

"I thought you kissed her once," she said, veiling her eyes behind her eyelashes.

"Only once?" The mockery in his voice made her blush. "Have you had anything to eat yet?" he went on.

"Not since lunchtime," she admitted. "Have you?"

He sighed. "What an exciting life you seem to think I lead," he said. "You wouldn't be in the least surprised if I told you

169

that I had eaten off gold plates, served by a half a dozen half-naked females, would you?"

"No," she said.

"Whereas the truth is that I didn't have any lunch and had to go to the University this afternoon to pick up some papers. And the only person I wish to entertain this evening is your fair self!"

She looked at him then, her eyes wide. "Oh Mark, yes, please!" she gasped.

He touched her very gently on the cheek. "Then we'll do the whole thing properly, my love. You'd better go and change your dress if you want to keep pace with the other fair charmers I've wined and dined, and I'll go and find Mihrimar and find out what delicacies she can produce for us." He gave her a push in the direction of the door. "Don't be long!" he warned her. "I want to talk to you."

She made no attempt to hide her pleasure. "D-do you?" she stammered. She swallowed, scarcely able to contain her excitement. First it had been darling, now it was his love! "What about?"

He leaned forward until his face was nearly touching hers. "Hurry up!" he commanded.

"Yes, yes, I will," she agreed hastily. "Mark —?"

"Hurry up!" he said again. 'I've done all the waiting I intend to do. With Ursula I put up with it, but wait for you I won't! If you're not ready in ten minutes, I'll come up and get you!"

"*Mark!*" she spluttered.

"Nine minutes," he amended.

She scooted out of the room and up the stairs, her heart pounding within her. It was a gorgeous evening, and she had never been so happy in her entire life, but supposing — supposing he was *only* going to wine and dine her? Supposing he didn't want her for ever and ever, amen? She didn't care, she told herself fiercely. She didn't care about anything. Tonight might never come again, she might never be as close to him again. Oh, she was right to make the most of it, and she would. She would take whatever he offered her and she would be grateful.

She surveyed her wardrobe with displeasure. She had nothing that she felt would really do justice to the occasion. She had no means of knowing what the other women of his acquaintance wore, but she guessed that they leaned towards the exotic, with expensive, champagne-and-caviar tastes like Ursula. No, she wouldn't think about Ursula!

A long dress? Yes, definitely a long dress was called for. She only had one and she took it out now with hands that trembled. It was made of soft, clinging wool in a vivid scarlet that accentuated the dark brown of her hair and eyes. It was not at all the sort of dress that she could have worn as Ursula's secretary and general dogsbody. She put it on lovingly, touching the material that clung to her shape and fell to her feet in classical folds. "Melâhat!" she said to her reflection in the looking-glass, and hoped that Mark would think so too.

Then she brushed her hair till it shone, smiling a little at herself. Anyone would think she was in love!

Mark was waiting for her in the sitting room when she went downstairs. He rose to his feet as she stood, waiting uncertainly in the doorway.

"My Melâhat." She couldn't quite make out whether it was a statement or a question and she didn't dare look at him to find out.

"Yes," she whispered.

For a long moment he stood quite still, saying nothing then he whirled into action, seating her with an old-fashioned courtesy on the sofa, and rushing out into the hall to call to Mihrimar that they were ready to eat. When he came back, she had risen and had gone over to the window, looking out across the Bosphorus at the lights of Istanbul.

"I wasn't quite ten minutes." she said.

"Long enough! I thought we'd eat by candlelight and then we'll talk."

"T-talk?" She turned and looked at him for the first time. He looked immensely handsome in his evening clothes. She felt a tight constriction in her throat at the sight of him. To-night he was every inch what she had first imagined him. Maruk Bey! His Turkish name resounded round her head.

"Yes, talk," he said gravely. "I want you to be very, very sure, Melâhat mine, because after tonight there will be no going back. Understand?"

Madeleine nodded, not understanding at all. She gave him an impudent smile. "I thought you said you were hungry?" she said.

CHAPTER XII

MADELEINE sat opposite Mark across the polished table, the light of the candles reflected in her eyes. Mihrimar fussed round them both, breaking into giggles of sheer delight whenever she looked at them. Her comments in Turkish were terse and, Madeleine suspected, earthy. She might not have come to this conclusion if the Turkish woman hadn't watched over every mouthful of food she ate, refusing to allow anything flavoured with garlic, or indeed anything stronger than lemon juice, to pass her lips.

Mark waited until Mihrimar had gone back to the kitchen and then he said: "Well, are you enjoying being entertained in my house?"

"Yes," Madeleine claimed uncertainly. His amusement was very hard to bear, even if he had pretended not to notice Mihrimar's more obvious sallies. "You're right about Turkey," she added. "It is a man's country!"

His eyes gleamed with laughter. "You don't look as though you mind too much," he observed.

If she had any pride she would mind, she thought. But her pride where he was concerned had long ago been buried under an avalanche of some quite different emotion.

"No," she said. She dropped her eyes to her plate and took a hasty sip of wine. "It was a marvellous meal! I don't think I could eat another thing!"

"Then it's time for the entertainment proper to begin, don't you think?"

She nodded, quite unable to say anything. When he stood up, she was aware that he was smiling tenderly at her, but

173

she couldn't bring herself to look back at him. She preceded him out of the room and into the sitting-room, hoping that the weakness that had unaccountably grasped her knees would go away when she sat down. The mockery with which Mark offered her a cigarette did nothing to help her self-control.

"No, thank you," she said. She never smoked and, though she was tempted to take one now, to give herself something to do with her hands, the thought of choking over the unaccustomed Turkish tobacco made her refusal sound sharper than she had intended. She watched Mark light his own cigarette and wished that she had one half of his *savoir faire*.

He turned suddenly, his face alight with mischief. "How would you like me to entertain you?"

Her mouth felt dry, but she would not let him see how easy it was to needle her. She leaned back, apparently very much at her ease. "What do you usually do?" she asked him.

His laughter was disconcerting. Could nothing put him in a dither?

"I think your imagination has already told you the answer to that," he smiled. He bent over her, putting a hand on either side of her, and kissed her lightly on the lips. Then, as suddenly, he was gone, seating himself on a distant chair.

"Tell me about your home in England," he said. "What did your parents think of Ursula whisking you out here?"

He had managed to wrong-foot her again. The last thing she wanted to talk about was her family and her normal existence in England. Just for tonight she had wanted to be someone quite different, a dazzling charmer of the kind that would appeal to Mark Adeney, not Madeleine Carvill who wasn't at all that sort of girl. And now here he was actually asking about her parents as though he really cared.

"They were pleased for me," she answered. "It all happened so quickly, but it was nice that I should have been picked out to go with Mrs. Adeney. We — we live quite near to London. Very ordinary. My parents don't like going abroad themselves, but they don't mind my going — as long as I come back again." She gave him a look of uncertainty. "They'll *never* understand!"

"Understand what?"

"Turkey. It's different from anything they've ever known. *I'm* different!" She blinked rapidly, appalled by what she was going to say. "I don't want to go home," she said baldly. "I want to stay here!"

She barely noticed the triumphant way he looked at her. "Then why don't you stay?" he asked. "I'm not driving you away."

"I can't! I'd never be able to get work in Istanbul and I can't live on nothing. And I can't go on staying here."

"Why not?" He was actually daring to laugh at her! "You didn't mind before?"

"But I did mind! I minded dreadfully! When you knew I was connected to Ursula, you didn't want to have anything more to do with me. You didn't want either of us!"

"I didn't want Ursula," he admitted.

"You didn't want me either!"

"That's all you know," he said dryly. "I thought I'd leave it for a day or so while I tied up the ends of my job with the University, but when I found you had broken into my own house, I knew I'd have to keep you here somehow, even if it did mean putting up with Ursula's nonsense."

Madeleine stared at him. "I didn't break into your house!" she objected.

"I don't care how you got in! You looked very inviting and I haven't been able to get you out of my heart and mind ever since!"

Madeleine's heart jerked with a new, blissful excitement. "You said I was beautiful," she remembered. Her mouth trembled into a smile. "I thought you were beautiful too. I mean, I still do! I think you look particularly nice tonight," she blurted out.

"Madeleine, this isn't a romantic dream to me –"

She was taken aback. "What have you got against romance?"

He made an exasperated movement. "Nothing. I'm all for it in its right place, but I'm not Maruk Bey, my dear, and wishing won't make me so."

"I know that!"

"Do you? Think hard, Madeleine. Do you know it? You called me Maruk Bey the other day!"

"Yes, I did," she admitted. "But only because it suits you, Mark. I know you're not Turkish, and even if you were, you wouldn't be – be –"

"Be what?"

She cast all discretion to the winds. "Wasn't there once a girl called Aimée, a cousin of Napoleon's Josephine, who was captured by corsairs and sent to the Sultan at Istanbul by the Bey of Algiers? The Sultan might never have noticed her, or he might have been as horrid as Selim the Sot, but he wasn't, and he did notice her, and she – she loved him!"

"What does that prove?" he asked her.

She took a deep breath, not looking at him. "I think it was romantic, and it happened to be true. Maruk Bey is a little bit true to me. I like it when he calls me Melâhat and – and –"

"Lets you know you're *gözde* as far as I'm concerned," he supplied.

"Well, yes," she said, unexpectedly grateful for his intervention. "Only it isn't enough! There must have been lots of times when Aimée wished that her Sultan were a more ordinary man, don't you think? They couldn't have had much *privacy*!"

"Ah," said Mark, "so you think a more bread and butter existence has its points?"

She nodded. "To be perfect, one would have both." She turned and faced him, a little white. "You are both to me – both Mark Adeney and Maruk Bey. I – I love both of you!"

"Oh, my little love!" he said in a tone of voice she had

never heard before. "I'm a brute, but I can't let you go!" He scooped her out of her seat and sat down where she had been sitting, pulling her down on to his knee. "Can you bear to stay in Istanbul for three years with me?"

"W-with you?"

He kissed her. "There must be some way of getting married here," he said.

She pulled away from him. "Marry you? But you don't want to marry anyone! If I could stay a little while, I'd try to be content with that. I know you'd want – other women, and I'll try not to mind. I mean, I shall mind, but I'll understand, truly I will. I do so want to be with you!"

He held her tightly against him. "That's why we'll get married," he said. "Anything else wouldn't be enough for *me*. I'm not going to pretend that I haven't had my fun, but one doesn't marry for amusement, sweetheart. I knew when I first saw you that you were something very special to me, but that's nothing to how I feel now. We're one flesh, whether we go through some ceremony or not, and I'd like to proclaim that to the whole world. I want to put my ring on your finger –"

"You want everyone to know that you own me!" she accused him.

He grinned, "Why not?"

"I think you ought to wear a wedding ring too!"

"I will if you like," he consented, still smiling.

She sighed. "It wouldn't be the same," she said. "When you first kissed me, you didn't care if I wanted to or not. It was marvellous!"

He kissed her ear. "Of course I knew!"

"I don't see how you could," she said. "I was too busy telling you that I wanted equality."

"Your lips were telling me something quite different. Besides," he added gently, "I'd seen your face when I said goodbye to you at the Galata Tower. You're not very good at hiding your feelings, are you?"

"I'd never met anyone like you," she confessed. "I can't believe it now!"

"That," he said, "is something we can do something about." His eyes glinted in a way that set her pulses racing. "It's been as much as I could do to keep my hands off you these last few days, and now, my love, I'm going to kiss you as much as I like. Any objections?"

She shook her head. "Would it matter if I had?" she smiled.

"Not a bit!" he said cheerfully. Her eyes widened as she saw the way he was looking at her, but then his lips came down on hers and the unfailing magic took possession of her, and she was beyond thought, beyond anything besides giving him the eager response that he demanded.

It was a long time later when he finally released her. "*I wonder, by my troth, what thou and I did, till we lov'd?*" he murmured against her throat. "I'm going to take you to a hotel, and you'll stay there until I can marry you. Is that clear?"

If she had doubted that he loved her, she would have known it then.

"Oh, Mark, thank you!" she said. "But I'll stay if you want me to?"

"No, I can wait. We can both wait until I can make you legally mine. I have an idea that you would regret anything else, and I would too. You'd better go and pack your bag."

She said nothing, but she took his hand in hers and kissed it. Then she hurried out of the room before either of them could change their minds.

Madeleine would not have believed that getting married could be such an exhausting business. The American Consulate, the British Consulate, the Turkish officials, the Protestant chaplain, all had to be consulted, persuaded, and cajoled into playing their parts. Madeleine wondered audibly whether it wouldn't be simpler to get the Greek Patriarch to marry them, once she had discovered that he lived in Istanbul, but this brought forth a united negative from everyone else.

"Pity," she said. "I rather fancied seeing Mark crowned. Besides, their churches are so splendid!"

The British official laughed amiably. "I believe the bride is crowned too," he remarked.

Madeleine cast Mark a malicious look. "But only as consort, I'm sure," she said, presenting a meek face. "Oh well, what can we do?"

The answer seemed to be to fill in forms. A mountain of papers was set before them, asking impossible questions to which neither of them had the remotest idea of the answers.

"Where are we going to live?" Madeleine asked Mark in the middle of all the chaotic activity about them

"Here, of course," he said.

"Yes, *now*. But where are we going to live in the end?" For a moment, the familiar, inscrutable look came over his face again.

"Where do you want to live?" He hesitated. "Do you want to go back to England?"

She shook her head. "I only want to be with you!"

"America?"

"If that's what you want," she said.

"I hadn't thought I was asking you to uproot yourself entirely. Do you mind?"

She forgot there were other people there. "You once said that if I were yours, I'd have to take what I was given and be grateful," she reminded him. "Don't you know yet that I'd follow you, gypsy fashion, right across the world! I'd even carry the luggage!"

He shook his head at her, laughing. "I knew there was some reason why I wanted to marry you! It was a porter I needed, of course! Oh, Melâhat, you'd better hurry up and finish those forms, or I'll forget all my good intentions and carry you off before we ever get to the end of this paperchase! Do you, by any chance, know your great-grandfather's Christian name?"

Madeleine considered the matter, her eyes mischievous. "On which side?" she asked.

"On any side!" he said in mock despair

But then, quite suddenly, it was all arranged. The blood tests had been taken, the forms filled in, the final arrangements made, and the day was upon them. There were two telegrams waiting for them from Madeleine's parents. Madeleine's read simply: Be happy. Lots of love. Mother and Father. The other, addressed to Mark, was only a little longer. Thank you, it said, for making our daughter happy.

The day before the wedding and the telegrams, Madeleine had received a cheque from the London office of Adeney Publications. At first glance it had seemed a great deal of money, but when she thought what she wanted to do with it, she knew it was only barely adequate.

It wasn't difficult to slip out of the hotel by herself and to walk down the steep hill to the Galata Bridge and over to the other side. Indeed, this time she had no difficulty in finding the covered bazaar and was soon wandering through the roofed-in, narrow streets, with their pocket-sized shops on either side. The reception clerk at the hotel had told her that the area she sought was roughly in the centre of the bazaar, but it took her a long time to find it When she did, a breath of excitement went through her and she pushed her way into the tiny shop.

"Hanimeffendi?"

Madeleine took a deep breath. "Do you speak English?"

"But of course, madame. How am I able to help you?"

Madeleine spilled the money she had changed into Turkish liras on to the narrow counter between her and the proprietor.

"I want an antique Koran. The very best you have."

The shopkeeper showed no sign of surprise. He appeared to have counted up the money at a glance. "It is for somebody special?" he suggested.

"Very special!"

"May one ask for whom?"

Madeleine gave him an anxious smile. "I'm marrying him tomorrow," she explained awkwardly. "This is my wedding present to him. He teaches at the University His name is Mark Adeney."

The shopkeeper's quick look of recognition pleased her. If he knew Mark, he would know of his interest in the ancient Turkish calligraphy.

"Maruk Bey is to receive this Koran?"

She nodded. "But that's all the money I have. It may not be enough –"

"It is enough."

He brought out a large, beautifully bound volume and laid it on the counter before her, turning the pages with such infinite care that Madeleine didn't dare touch it at all. The calligraphy was old, older than the flowing script that decorated the Istanbulu mosques. It was stiff and upright, with separate letters, such as she remembered seeing in the Islamic museum in the old Spanish Korans from Cordova.

"This one is worthy of Maruk Bey," the man murmured lovingly. "He has knowledge of these things and is not to be deceived by one of lesser value."

"But it's worth much more than I can pay!" Madeleine answered. "That's all the money I have!"

"I told you, it is enough," the man smiled.

He clapped his hands and called for tea, which he suggested that Madeleine should drink while he packed up the Koran, ready for her to take away. Madeleine thanked him in her few words of Turkish, as she felt it would be more courteous to at least try to address him in his own language. He gave her an interested look and smiled again.

"At least tea is a easy word to remember in any language," he said. "It is said there were two Chinese traders who dealt in tea, dividing the world between them. That is why those

181

who were sold tea by Mr. Chai call it after him, and those by Mr. Te, or Ti, call it by his name. In Istanbul we were in the centre of world trade and had many dealings with both east and west, but we call our tea after Mr. Chai."

Madeleine carried the Koran carefully back to the hotel with her. She hoped Mark wouldn't be angry that he would have to pay her hotel bill for her, but she thought the ancient book would more than make it up to him. She hugged it to her under her coat, to protect it from the spitting rain. Tomorrow would be fine, she thought. She gave a quick skip of pleasure and hurried on her way.

The morning dawned as fine as she had wished. It was still early when the British Consul came to fetch her, and it was he who paid her bill at the hotel, dismissing her embarrassment at not being able to do so herself. She showed him the Koran she had bought for Mark and, although it was clearly not something he wanted himself, he was suitably impressed and even carried it for her to the car.

"By the way," he said as they drove away, "I have a copy of the English language newspaper for you. It mentions your recent employer and her fiancé. I thought you might be interested."

She looked down at the column where he was pointing and read the notice.

Mrs. Ursula Adeney is to marry Colonel Oliver Welland next week. They have been friends since childhood and the marriage comes as no surprise to their many friends. Colonel Welland is in Turkey as the American representative to the recent N.A.T.O. discussions held in Ankara. Mrs. Adeney is the owner of the powerful magazine chain, Adeney Publications. She said yesterday she had no intention of selling the magazines left to her by her first husband. As her fiancé will be away a great deal on Army business, she will have plenty of time to continue with all her former interests in the literary and political worlds of the United States.

So, Madeleine thought, Ursula had won after all, if that was what she wanted. For a minute she could have wept for her, for anyone who wasn't as happy as she was herself that day, but then the moment passed and she stepped out of the car, knowing that Mark was waiting for her.

When at last she was left alone with her husband, Madeleine felt as shy of him as she had that very first day when she had first seen him in the harem of the Topkapi Palace.

"I promised Mihrimar we wouldn't return until evening," he told her. "She has all her friends in, cleaning the *yali* from top to bottom in your honour. I left them weaving spells to keep the evil spirits away from our marriage bed!"

Madeleine blushed. She thrust her wedding present into his hands and tried to school her tongue into saying something appropriate. But she could think of nothing. "I haven't a penny in the world!" she burst out "I do hope you won't mind, Mark, but I spent it all on this!"

He unwrapped the parcel carefully. "Is this why I had to pay the British Consul for your hotel bill before he would allow the ceremony to proceed?" he teased her with all his usual mockery. The paper fell away to reveal the hand-wrought cover of the Koran and his smile suddenly died, giving way to the old inscrutable expression she knew so well.

"I wanted to give you something special," Madeleine said quickly. "I wanted to give you a symbolic return for all you've given me. Oh, Mark, you don't like it!"

"It's perfect," he said.

She studied his face anxiously. "I wanted to give you something special," she said again.

He looked at her then. "You don't know how special it is," he said intensely. "I never hoped to own anything half as beautiful as this! Darling, I adore it, and I adore you for giving it to me! You see, I saw it in the bazaar a few days ago, but I hadn't nearly enough to buy it. How did you manage it?"

183

Madeleine attempted a smile. "I had my cheque from Adeney Publications. I don't think it was nearly enough either, but he insisted that I take it when he knew who it was for. Mark, you really do like it, don't you?"

"Next to you, there's nothing I've ever wanted more!" he told her.

Madeleine's relief was obvious. "Show me where it says that men are superior to women," she demanded.

He had to admit that he couldn't himself read the old script, but he showed her approximately where it came, counting out the various chapters. "The Opening Surah; the Surah of the Heifer; the Surah of the Imran's family; the Surah of Women. It comes somewhere in that."

"You really meant that and – and the other quotation that night, didn't you?" she accused him.

He grinned. "And if I did?"

"It isn't all it says," she said knowledgeably. "It is also written 'If ye be kind to women and fear to wrong them, God is well acquainted with what ye do.'"

"Does it indeed?" His eyes mocked her. "Did you think me unkind to tell you your place in life?"

She refused to meet his eyes, knowing that he was laughing at her. "No," she said. "It was the first time I admitted to myself that I was in love with you. You were wonderful! Only I was afraid you didn't want me – on a permanent basis –"

"Oh, lord," he exclaimed. "Where can we go so that I can kiss you in peace?"

Madeleine looked at him shyly through her lashes. "May we go to Eyüp?"

"If you like. But not on the bus, my Melâhat! I intend to have you all to myself this afternoon and not share you with half the population of Istanbul. We'll take a taxi all the way." He put an affectionate arm about her shoulders, his eyes laughing at her. "Are you going to make another wish at the Window of Mercy?"

She held his hand tightly. "No, I want to thank him. My wish came true, you see."

"Did it?" His voice was so gentle that she found she didn't mind him knowing what she had wished for, though she was almost sure he already knew. "I made a request that day myself," he went on. "I asked him to make you mine!"

"But you knew –" she began, and broke off.

"Yes, I knew," he agreed.

"Then why?"

"I was afraid you were in love with Maruk Bey and not at all with me –"

"But now you know better?"

"Darling, at this moment I don't care!"

She gave way easily to the pressure of his arms, tipping her face eagerly to meet his kiss. It was a long time coming. He touched her mouth with a finger, following the line of her jaw and running his hand through the soft curtain of her hair.

"I love you, Melâhat," he said huskily.

When he kissed her he was not at all gentle, but she didn't care. She wound her arms round his neck and with a little sob of pure pleasure gave him back kiss for kiss. The sweet, familiar sensation of weakness and submission made her cling to him all the harder. When he finally put her away from him, she muttered a soft protest accompanied by a shaky laugh.

"And I love you!" she said.

The sunshine lit the courtyard of the mosque at Eyüp, with only the shadows of the trees to give relief from the blinding whiteness. The pigeons cooed to one another, their bright eyes greedy for the food the pilgrims put down for them. The larger birds, the wounded storks and the occasional heron, stood shyly to one side, as if afraid of the crowds of human beings who pressed forward to their goal of standing before the small window let into the *türbe* of the Prophet's friend and standard-bearer.

Madeleine and Mark joined the queue, their hands linked as

they waited in silence for their turn at the Window of Pity. The blues and mauves of the tiles reflected the sun with a glare that hurt their eyes. Then, at last, their turn came. Madeleine grasped the brass fretwork with her fingers and offered her thanks, aware of Mark's amusement as he watched her.

"You never did say what you were thanking him for," he reminded her as they walked slowly away.

"No," she said "He gave me more than I asked for. I asked only that you would love me – more than anyone else. I never thought you'd marry me."

"You underrate yourself," he said dryly.

She laughed. "No, I don't, but I didn't know what to expect –"

"And you do now?"

"I think so. But I shall never cease to give thanks all the same. I've never done anything to deserve you, and I probably never shall, but I will try to be all you want all my life long."

"You are all I want, all I shall ever want –"

She cut him off with a quick kiss. "I'm thirsty," she complained. "Let's walk up to that café that looks over the Golden Horn and have some tea while we watch the sun set. I want to be kissed again in the moonlight and then I want to go home – with you!"

From the café they could see the waters of first the Horn and then the Bosphorus turn to liquid gold. The pencil-slim minarets stood out amongst the domes right across the sky-line, but they had eyes for nothing but each other. There would be many other nights to watch the sun set over Istanbul, but this was their night for loving Thinking of how Mark had quoted John Donne to her when he had asked her to marry him, Madeleine found the words of the poet came unbidden to her mind. She was scarcely aware that she had spoken them aloud, but she was glad that she had, when she saw her husband's face light up.

"Tonight puts on perfection, and a woman's name."

This month's
Harlequin
Romances

Every month eight great new stories in the world's most popular series of romances.

| No. 1753 | Nan Asquith | No. 1757 | Dorothy Cork |
| TIME MAY CHANGE | | THE GIRL AT SALTBUSH FLAT | |

| No. 1754 | Lucy Gillen | No. 1758 | Elizabeth Hunter |
| THE PRETTY WITCH | | THE CRESCENT MOON | |

| No. 1755 | Penelope Walsh | No. 1759 | Marjorie Lewty |
| SCHOOL MY HEART | | THE REST IS MAGIC | |

| No. 1756 | Kay Thorpe | No. 1760 | Katrina Britt |
| AN APPLE IN EDEN | | THE GUARDED GATES | |

Still only 60¢ each
Harlequin
Presents ...
75¢ each

No. 34   Stormy The Way
ANNE HAMPSON

No. 35   Seen By Candlelight
ANNE MATHER

No. 36   Love's Prisoner
VIOLET WINSPEAR

All titles available at your local store. If unable to obtain titles of your choice, you may order from

HARLEQUIN READER SERVICE
M.P.O. Box 707
Niagara Falls, N.Y. 14302
Canadian address:
Stratford, Ontario, Canada.

F R E E ! ! !
Did you know . . . . . . ?

that just by mailing in the coupon below you can receive a
brand new, up-to-date "Harlequin Romance Catalogue"
listing literally hundreds of Harlequin Romances you
probably thought were out of print.

Now you can shop in your own home for novels by your
favorite Harlequin authors — the Essie Summers you
wanted to read, the Violet Winspear you missed, the Mary
Burchell you thought wasn't available anymore!

They're all listed in the "Harlequin Romance Catalogue".
And something else too — the books are listed in numerical
sequence, — so you can fill in the missing numbers in your
library.

Don't delay — mail the coupon below to us today. We'll
promptly send you the "Harlequin Romance Catalogue"

F R E E !

A Treasury of Harlequin Romances!

Golden Harlequin Library

Many of the all time favorite Harlequin Romance Novels have not been available, until now, since the original printing. But now they are yours in an exquisitely bound, rich gold hardcover with royal blue imprint. Three complete unabridged novels in each volume. And the cost is so very low you'll be amazed!

Handsome, Hardcover Library Editions at Paperback Prices! ONLY $1.95 each volume.

SPECIAL INTRODUCTORY OFFER!

Order volumes No. 1, 2, 3, 4 and 5 now and get volume No. 6 FREE! Just imagine . . . 18 unabridged HARLEQUIN ROMANCES beautifully bound in six library editions for only $9.75.

Start your collection now. See reverse of this page for brief story outlines of the FIRST SIX volumes.

To: HARLEQUIN READER SERVICE, Dept. G 402
M.P.O. Box 707 Niagara Falls, N.Y. 14302
Canadian address: Stratford, Ont., Canada

☐ Please send me the free Harlequin Romance Catalogue.

☐ Please send me the Golden Harlequin Library editions I have checked.

I enclose $_____ (No C.O.D.'s) To help defray postage and handling costs, please add 50c.

NAME . . . .

ADDRESS . . . .

CITY/TOWN. . . . .

STATE/PROV. . . . . ZIP . . . .

Golden Harlequin $1.95 per vol.

Each Volume Contains 3 Complete Harlequin Romances

Golden Harlequin $1.95 per vol.

Each Volume Contains 3 Complete Harlequin Romances

☐ Volume 3

FAIR HORIZON by Rosalind Brett   760

An ordinary English girl and a beautiful, sophisticated Swedish widow vie for the love of a successful man in this exciting story set in Kenya.

DESERT NURSE by Jane Arbor   801

Martha Shore successfully managed to jump out of the "frying pan"— but her new job in the burning desert heat east of Aden began, ominously, to resemble the proverbial fire!

QUEENS COUNCIL by Alex Stuart   506

Charles spoke aloud the vows which would make Linda his wife. But tragedy brooded over the quiet, flower-decked church. A tragedy he could not share with her.

☐ Volume 4

THE YOUNGEST BRIDESMAID by Sara Seale   816

When Melissa walked out on him, Piers asked Linda to marry him instead. Melissa had other ideas, and on the honeymoon she began to put them into practice.

DO SOMETHING DANGEROUS by Elizabeth Hoy   501

Sally wanted adventure and danger as assistant purser on the "Ocean Queen". She did encounter water, gales and fire, — and the unforseen, incalculable risks of falling in love.

DOCTOR DAVID ADVISES by Hilary Wilde   875

After being jilted Clare left for Australia on a six month nursing job. Then she had to go and fall in love again — on the rebound!

Golden Harlequin $1.95 per vol.

Each Volume Contains 3 Complete Harlequin Romances